"Wow! Look, ~~W~~ *You're on TV!" Wis* ~~...~~ *...*

"Oh, my." Wanda smiled as she caught a glimpse of herself. "It's from today's interview." She stared happily at the screen until the picture changed to anchorperson Helen Davidson, in the TV station's newsroom.

"Wanda Gilmore: local hero—or town tyrant?" Helen Davidson asked. "Things may not be as they appear for the Oakdale hero. Learn about her secrets and backroom dealings in Mitch McCain's exclusive investigative report, tomorrow on Fast News Fifty-seven."

"That guy is really, really, really bad news," Wishbone said, watching Wanda as her mouth dropped open in surprise. He nosed her hand. "Wanda? Wanda, are you okay?"

The SUPER Adventures of WISHBONE™

WISHBONE'S Dog Days OF THE WEST

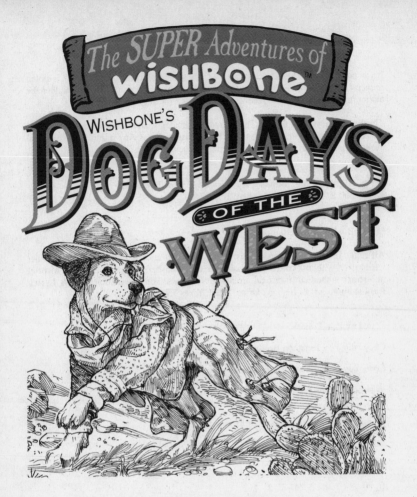

by Vivian Sathre

Screen story by Rick Duffield and Susan B. Chick

Screenplay by Susan B. Chick, Steven Kavner, and Michael Anthony Steele

Inspired by *Heart of the West* by O. Henry

WISHBONE™ created by Rick Duffield

Big Red Chair Books™, *A Division of* **Lyrick Publishing**™

This book is a work of fiction. The characters, incidents, and dialogues are products of the author's imagination and are not to be construed as real. Any resemblance to actual events or persons, living or dead, is entirely coincidental.

 Big Red Chair Books™, *A Division of Lyrick Publishing*™
300 E. Bethany Drive, Allen, Texas 75002

©1998 Big Feats! Entertainment

Edited by Pam Pollack

Copy edited by Jonathon Brodman

Cover design and interior illustrations by Lyle Miller

Wishbone photograph by Carol Kaelson

Library of Congress Catalog Card Number: 97-81411

ISBN: 1-57064-336-9

First printing: June 1998

10 9 8 7 6 5 4 3 2 1

In memory of my father, Bruce Kapuscinski,
who occasionally sneaked home a puppy
in a cardboard box,
and to my mother, Margaret,
who always let us keep it

FROM THE BIG RED CHAIR . . .

Oh . . . hi! Wishbone here. You caught me right in the middle of some of my favorite things—books. Let me welcome you to THE SUPER ADVENTURES OF WISHBONE. In each of these books, I have adventures with my friends in Oakdale and imagine myself as a character in one of the greatest stories of all time. This story takes place in the summer, when Joe is fourteen and he and his friends are about to enter ninth grade—during the second season of my television show. In *WISHBONE'S DOG DAYS OF THE WEST*, I imagine I'm "Long" Bill Longley, cowboy turned bank manager, from O. Henry's *HEART OF THE WEST—* a great collection of stories about life in America's Old West.

You're in for a real treat, so pull up a chair and a snack and sink your teeth into *WISHBONE'S DOG DAYS OF THE WEST!*

Chapter One

Sunshine warmed his back as Wishbone, the white-with-brown-and-black-spots Jack Russell terrier, trotted down Oak Street on a fine Sunday afternoon. The people of Oakdale stood around him, enjoying the games, rides, and entertainment.

"Ah, the summer carnival!" Wishbone admired the green balloon that his best friend, Joe Talbot, secured to his leash. Then he leaned forward and tugged to move ahead. "Joe, Ellen, can't you two walk any faster? You have four legs between the two of you." When they continued at their slow pace, Wishbone tugged harder. "You know, Joe, now that you're going into ninth grade, you're really hard to pull around."

Joe's mom, Ellen, cocked her head as the words to "America, the Beautiful" floated through

the air. "Isn't that Melina Finch singing?" she asked.

"I think so," Joe said, looking over the heads of the people who were gathering around the stage. He slowed to make way for a clown on stilts.

"Whoa!" Wishbone stepped back and looked way up high to the white-painted face with the big red nose. "Joe, maybe you should recruit this guy for your basketball team."

They walked past people of every size and shape dressed in bright summer clothes. Suddenly, Joe and Ellen stopped and joined a crowd of onlookers.

Wishbone poked his head through the forest of legs and saw a performer juggling three bowling pins. "That's nothing, pal. You should see what I can do with my squeaky toys."

Wishbone tugged against his leash. It was hard to keep Joe and Ellen focused. There was so much to see.

"Come on, Joe. Look around. Kids are running every which way. . . . They're free, Joe . . . unleashed! And they have caramel apples, doughnuts, and onion burgers. This is the great American celebration of freedom, fun, and food."

Joe didn't budge, so Wishbone tugged harder.

"Right now I seem to be having a little difficulty with the freedom issue."

Finally, Joe and Ellen stepped into the flow of people again. "Easy, Wishbone," Joe said, holding him back. "I know you don't like being on a leash, but there's too much going on today for you to be running around by yourself."

Wishbone wagged his tail. "But that's what carnivals are all about, Joe—running around free, and maybe getting *fed* for free. That's what I've been trying to tell you." Wishbone tried to follow a young boy with a dripping ice-cream cone. When the leash brought him to a sudden halt, he sighed and glanced back at Joe. "As usual, no one's listening to a word the dog is saying."

"Oh, look." Ellen pointed up the street. "There's Sam and Walter's booth."

"Pizza!" Wishbone called. He crossed with Joe and Ellen to Pepper Pete's Pizza Parlor booth. "And the Keplers make the best in town. Take it from me, the experienced and famous food critic."

Besides that, Samantha Kepler was one of Joe's best friends, and she almost always offered her favorite canine a friendly scratch or two. *And* they sort of had something in common—Sam had something like a tail. A blond *pony*tail.

Wishbone wagged his tail as his family neared Sam's. "Hi, Sam. Hi, Walter."

"Hi," Ellen called, waving to Sam and her dad. "Nice hats." She nodded to the red-white-and-green chef hats atop their heads.

"Hi, guys," Joe chimed in. Using his hand, he shielded his eyes from the sun. "How's it going?"

A smile lit up Walter's face. "The pizza's selling great. You can't live on corn dogs alone, you know."

Wishbone took a step back. "Now what, exactly, are corn dogs made of?"

Sam's glance shifted to the left. "Look at the bounce house." She pointed.

Joe, Ellen, Walter, and Wishbone turned toward the big, blue, inflatable room that was wriggling and jiggling. Laughter spilled from the flaplike doorway.

"It's been so much fun just watching kids jumping inside there," Sam said. "You take off your shoes, go in, and bounce on the floor. Somebody said it's like jumping on a water bed."

"Cool." Joe grinned.

Sam removed her hat. "You want to try it, Joe?"

"Yes!" Wishbone wagged his tail excitedly. "I vote that we all go try it!"

Joe held the leash out to Ellen. "Mom, will you watch Wishbone?"

"Sure." Ellen took the leash.

"Too bad David and his family are on vacation," Joe said. "I bet David would really like this thing."

Sam slipped her apron off. "You're right."

"Hey!" Wishbone watched Joe and Sam hurry toward the bounce house. "Don't I get to go? I thought we were *all* best friends."

Ellen gently tugged the leash. "Come on, Wishbone. Let's go listen to some music." She smiled. "See you later, Walter."

"Okay." Walter went back to his pizza-making chores.

"But I voted," Wishbone said, not moving. "This is America—where freedom rings and voting counts!" He looked up and saw Ellen's impatient expression. "Okay, I'll go—but not with great relish. How about if we share a slice of pizza first?"

Ellen steered Wishbone back into the foot traffic.

"That's a 'no,' isn't it?" he asked.

They reached the sandy area surrounding the stage just as Melina's song came to an end. "Darn! I missed it," Ellen said, applauding with the other onlookers.

"So, that's the glee club," Wishbone said. He tilted his head as he looked at the kids onstage. "Eleven-year-olds in matching yellow shirts." He looked at the younger kids playing in the sand below the singers. "Buckets? Shovels? Oh, I get it. It's a fake beach! Well, with all this sand, I hope someone put up a 'No Cats Allowed' sign."

Smiling, Ellen walked over to Travis Del Rio, the owner of Oakdale Sports & Games. Travis was standing nearby with his nephew, Marcus. "Hi, Travis. Melina has such a beautiful voice."

Travis nodded proudly as he watched his niece. "Thank you."

Wishbone looked up. He had to admire Travis. The man was a sports fan, and he had traveled a lot to participate in athletic events. Then, when Travis's sister and her husband were killed in a car accident, Travis decided to adopt his niece and nephew. So he opened Oakdale Sports & Games as a way to still stay around sports, and also to set up a stable home-life for his kids. He and Melina and Marcus moved into an apartment above the store. Wishbone got excited just thinking about owning all the balls in Travis's store—basketballs, soccer balls, tennis balls. He could choose a new one every morning!

"I think Melina's about to sing her second solo," Travis said.

"Oh, great." Ellen looked at Marcus, Melina's ten-year-old brother. "Are you going to join the glee club next year?"

"No way." He kneeled down to pet Wishbone.

"Marcus!" Wishbone wagged his tail. "I'm a political prisoner. I didn't do anything wrong. Really. They're just holding me captive because I'm a dog." He lowered his voice. "Now unhook that little clippy thing on the right side of my collar and set me free."

Marcus scratched under Wishbone's chin. "You like that, don't you, boy?" He looked at Ellen. "Mrs. Talbot, can I take Wishbone around the carnival?"

Ellen glanced over at Travis. When he nodded his approval, she handed the leash to Marcus. "Sure." She leaned down and smiled. "No cotton candy, Wishbone."

Wishbone couldn't believe his canine ears, even though his hearing was nothing short of amazing. "No cotton candy? Oh, this is going *too* far, Ellen. You—"

"Come on, Wishbone." As Marcus pulled him away, Ellen and Travis turned back to face the stage to wait for Melina to start her song.

Dodging feet, Wishbone walked through the carnival grounds with Marcus. He held his head high. "I am a dog living in the United States. I have rights. Freedom of speech. Freedom of treats. Freedom to go outside when I need to."

Marcus pulled Wishbone to a stop in front of the *Oakdale Chronicle* building. That was where Wanda Gilmore, Wishbone's neighbor and owner of the town's newspaper, was organizing the Oakdale Historical Society booth.

"Hi, Miss Gilmore. What are you doing with all the stuff on the table?" Marcus asked.

Wishbone took the leash in his teeth and sat down quietly. *If I stay real still, maybe she won't notice me. That pansy I trampled in her backyard was an accident. She can ask the flamingo. He saw the whole incident.*

"Well, hello, Marcus." Wanda looked up from the table. "The historical society keeps its things here"—she gestured behind her—"in the *Chronicle*

14

building. I'm setting up a miniature museum full of Oakdale artifacts."

Hank Dutton, Joe's classmate and an intern at the newspaper, pushed his way out the *Chronicle*'s door. He placed the box he was carrying on the table next to Wanda. "Here's the last of them, Miss Gilmore." He brushed the dust off the *Oakdale Chronicle* T-shirt he was wearing. "Hi, Marcus."

"Hi."

"Thank you, Hank." Wanda smiled appreciatively from under her multicolored striped straw hat. "And be sure to thank your grandfather for letting us borrow so many family treasures. I'm just sorry he didn't want to come to the carnival. Oh, well. I guess having all of this"—her hand waved over the table—"is the next-best thing to having Ethan Johnstone himself here."

Marcus brushed a bug from his leg and shot a glance at the bounce house.

"Are you enjoying the carnival?" Wanda asked, as she set out a baseball and mitt from the 1935 Oakdale Oaks Negro League.

Nodding, Marcus gave the inflated bounce house another long look. "I love the games and rides."

"Helllooo!" Wishbone couldn't sit still any longer. "How come no one's asking the tied-up little dog if he's enjoying the— *Ptew!*" He spat the leash out of his mouth. "As I was saying, the carnival."

As Hank's eyes followed Marcus's gaze, he smiled. "Have you been in the bounce house yet?"

Marcus perked up. "Not yet. Want to go?"

Hank cleared away an empty box and put it under the table. "Sorry. I promised Miss Gilmore I'd work the booth right now." He checked his watch. "I might hit it after my shift is over, though."

As Melina started her song, Wanda hummed along and stacked historical society pamphlets on the table.

Marcus glanced toward the bounce house and sighed. A second later he cheered up. "Miss Gilmore, will you watch Wishbone for a minute?" He held out the leash to her.

Wanda frowned and held up her hands to protest. "Well, I don't know—"

In an instant, Marcus had passed the leash to her. "Thanks, Miss Gilmore!" He rushed off. "I've just *got* to try the bounce house. . . ." His voice trailed back to them.

"Marcus, wait!" Wishbone begged. "Take me with you. Believe me, Wanda has never been filled with a great deal of love for dogs."

Wishbone looked up at Wanda's end of the leash and wagged his tail.

"Wanda, you don't want to hold on to that. It's got dog germs all over it."

Making a face, Wanda held the leash out as if she had the tail of a dead mouse pinched between her fingers.

"Dog germs," Wishbone repeated.

Wanda tried to hold the leash farther away, but her arm wouldn't stretch any more. "Wishbone, why don't we go find Ellen?" She looked at Hank. "Hold down the fort, will you, Hank?"

"Great idea!" Wishbone trotted ahead, leading Wanda toward the stage. "We'll go get Ellen and I'll present a list of demands. Demand number one: Remove Wanda from the end of my leash."

Wishbone sidestepped a running toddler.

"Demand number two: Remove Wishbone from the other end of the leash."

Wishbone looked up. His balloon had broken free and was rising high into the sky.

"Demand number three: a new green balloon for the cute, smart, and ever-faithful Jack Russell terrier."

As they passed the bounce house, Wishbone looked around.

"Ellen!" he called over Melina's singing.

At the grassy area on the side of the stage, Wanda stopped to watch Melina sing her solo. She pulled Wishbone to a sudden halt.

"Hey!" Wishbone gasped, his collar squeezing his neck. "Ellen . . . Ellen, where are you?"

Suddenly, as he looked over the crowd, the fur on his back bristled.

"Something's wrong, Wanda. I can feel it in my bones. Now, if I could only see it with my eyes."

Scritch.

Wishbone tried to identify where the sound came from, but it had happened too quickly. He perked up his ears and waited. Before long, his keen hearing picked up another low, slow *s-c-r-i-t-c-h*. His eyes rose to the wire cables that ran up behind the stage and connected to the overhead lights. Halfway up, one line had begun to fray.

Creak. It frayed a little more.

"Oh, no!" Wishbone bolted toward the stage, barking, dragging Wanda behind him.

Scritch.

"Look, Wanda!" Wishbone tugged against the leash. "Hurry! It's this thing right here." He pointed his nose at the cable to show her.

Wanda's mouth fell open as she stared at the fraying line in disbelief. The leash dropped from her hand.

Wishbone raced onto the stage, barking. He tried to herd the kids to one side. "Move off the stage in an orderly fashion. This is *not* a drill," he warned.

The kids looked at him, confused. Finally, they stopped singing and stepped back. Above them the lighting grid shook.

A murmur rose from the crowd in front of the stage. People looked up toward the grid. Some of the parents scooped their children out of the sand and darted to safety.

From the corner of his eye, Wishbone saw two men—one in a brown jacket, and one carrying a big TV camera—push their way through the crowd.

Suddenly, from beside the stage, Wanda whispered, "Oh, no! Melina!"

Wishbone heard the cable snap.

The kids looked up. The crowd of onlookers gasped as they saw the lighting grid drop on one side and sway.

"Get off the stage!" someone yelled.

"Never mind about being orderly." Wishbone barked. "Run!" He rushed off stage with the wide-eyed singers. But Melina still stood center front, frozen as she stared at the grid above her.

"Melina, look out!" Wanda bolted up onto the stage behind Melina, her eyes opened wide. She rushed forward, swooping Melina into her

arms and then swiftly jumping to the ground. A split-second later the lighting grid crashed onto the stage.

The crowd pushed forward. The man in the brown jacket was right there and had a microphone in Wanda's face. "Ma'am! Are you all right?" Next to him, the cameraman had the TV camera rolling.

"What?" Looking a bit confused and shaken, Wanda rubbed her left wrist.

"I'm a reporter—Mitch McCain. I'm with Fast News Fifty-seven." He cocked his head. "Say, aren't you Wanda Gilmore? Don't you own *The Oakdale Chronicle?*"

Wanda nodded. "Uh . . . yes . . ." She turned to Melina, sitting beside her in the sand.

Looking into the camera, Mitch changed his expression to a very professional one. Then he spoke into the microphone. "This is a frightening scene." He held the microphone out to Wanda. "Are you all right, ma'am?"

"I'm all right. . . ." She turned to Melina, concerned. "Are you all right, dear?"

Melina wriggled her foot. Her long, dark ponytail fell forward as she shook her head. "Yes. I'm okay, Miss Gilmore."

Mitch pulled the mike back to himself.

"Wanda . . . may I call you 'Wanda'? How did you know the accident was going to happen?"

She wrinkled her brows, puzzled. "Well . . . I didn't. I didn't, but Wishbone, here, did. He . . . he's the real hero here."

Before Wishbone knew it, the camera was pointed at his tail. "Hey." He turned two steps to the right. "At least show my good side."

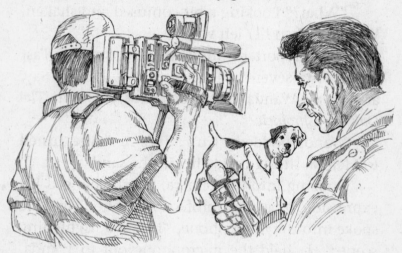

Shoving their way through opposite sides of the crowd, Travis and Ellen, and Sam, Joe, and Marcus, rushed up and circled Melina and Wanda. Travis kneeled by Melina. "Are you all right?" Mitch motioned the cameraman to film the scene.

"Want me to go and get you a soft drink or something?" Marcus asked.

Melina shook her head. "No, thanks."

Marcus looked at his uncle. "Is she hurt? Does she need to go to the doctor?"

Travis gently moved Melina's foot in a circle. "She'll be fine. I think she's just a little shaken up, that's all."

Ellen reached out and helped Wanda up. "Are you okay? That crash was horrifying."

Mitch snapped his fingers at the cameraman, who immediately aimed the camera at Mitch. "She saved the day," Mitch said into the mike. "What could have been a tragic event was prevented by a brave and quick-thinking woman. From the Oakdale summer carnival, this is Mitch McCain, for Fast News Fifty-seven." He smiled. "Remember, when you're looking for news, look for Mitch McCain."

Wanda touched Mitch McCain's shoulder. "Excuse me . . ." she said, trying to get his attention.

He turned to her, frowning at the interruption.

"No. No. I couldn't have done anything without Wishbone, here. He is just such an amazing dog!"

"'Amazing dog'—that's my cue." Wishbone trotted over and stood beside Joe.

Mitch looked him over. "Hmm . . . he is, isn't he?"

"That's right!" Wishbone said. "You see what I can do when no one's holding me by a leash?"

Mitch picked up the leash and looked at it for

a moment. "Yeah. We gotta be sure we get a good shot of this animal. You know, this is exactly the kind of story the TV network's looking for." He grabbed the leash in the middle to shorten Wishbone's lead.

"Hey, let go!" Wishbone eyed him suspiciously. "Not just anybody holds my leash." He tugged. When the leash slipped through the man's fingers, Wishbone bolted through the crowd. "I am outta here!"

"Hey, wait!" Mitch called.

Wishbone kept running. But before he got out of earshot, he heard Mitch tell Wanda she could see herself on the news that night. "Excuse me. Pardon me. One side. Coming through. Pardon me." As he squeezed past the juggler, the fellow dropped his pins. "Oops! Terribly sorry."

Finally, Wishbone was out of the crowded carnival area and all alone. Slowing, he walked down Oak Street.

"I tell you, leashes are the curse of modern civilization! No great hero ever lived on a leash. Was Davy Crockett ever on a leash? No. Wyatt Earp? No." Wishbone broke into a trot. "What about Daniel Boone?" He stopped. "Or John Wayne. Hey . . ."

Wishbone perked up his ears.

"I hear music." He trotted over to Snook's

Furniture Store, the source of the sound, and looked in the window. "Wow! Three televisions in one room." He sat on the sidewalk and watched the sets. An opening scene for an old western showed on all three screens. "A movie!" He tried to look past the sets in the window. "I wonder if this place serves buttered popcorn."

Wishbone sat back, scratched his ear, and watched dust and a tumbleweed blow across the screens.

"The Wild West—now, those were the good old days, when an honest dog was free to roam the open plains."

An actor dressed in leather chaps and vest, and sitting atop a horse, rode across the televisions and into a deserted town. He wore a tan cowboy hat, a brown neckerchief, and well-worn cowboy boots with spurs on them. Stopping at an old hitching rail, he dismounted and tied up his horse.

"Look at that!" Wishbone wagged his tail. "Back then it was the *horses* that were kept on a leash!"

Wishbone continued to watch the trio of screens. The actor reached into his saddlebag and removed a dark, leather-bound book. The word *journal* was imprinted across the front cover.

A gust of wind stirred the dust and caught

the cover of the book, flipping it open. On the first page, written in cursive, was the title: *Heart of the West: Short Stories by O. Henry.* Sitting down on the old wooden boardwalk that ran in front of the deserted stores behind him, the actor turned to another page. Then looking skyward in thought, he practiced his lines out loud before writing them in his book. "In those days the cattlemen were the admired ones. . . . They might have ridden in golden chariots, had they the desire to do so."

Fascinated, Wishbone stared at the TVs. The cowboy faded out and the picture changed to the open range. Wishbone sighed.

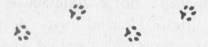

A cattleman living in the Old West, driving huge herds across the vast plains of Texas. Now, that's what I call an adventure. . . . Yee-haw! Get along, little dogie!

The writer William Sydney Porter (1862–1910), who is known by his pen name—writing name— O. Henry, liked the Old West, too. O. Henry moved from North Carolina to Texas and actually worked as a cowboy so he could experience firsthand the magic of the West.

But the days of the cowboy were giving way to modern times. Boomtowns that had sprung up during the gold-rush days of 1849 to 1854 became ghost towns. O. Henry, however, wanted to capture, for all time, the spirit of the untamed American West. He wrote a collection of short stories and called them *Heart of the West*.

Chapter Two

So Wishbone imagined himself as Long Bill Longley, a character in one of O. Henry's short stories.

Long Bill was a cowboy legend who cast a giant shadow across the Wild West. The cattle boom of the 1880s had caught Long Bill in a stampede of dollars, making him a baron of beef and bone. With his success, Long Bill built a small, but nice, house close to the little frontier town of Chaparosa, Texas. Because of his wealth, he was expected to become a leading citizen of the town. So Long Bill hung up his chaps, retired as a cowboy, and opened the First National Bank of Chaparosa, and became bank president.

Long Bill pawed the derby hat on his head into place. Giving himself a good shake, he loosened his necktie—just enough so it still looked neat. Then he leaped from the front porch of his house up to the top of his covered rain barrel. With another push from his hind legs, he jumped up into his saddle.

"Steady, girl."

Sitting atop his horse, Ginger, Long Bill could see a whole lot of Texas—flat, dusty, and dotted with sagebrush. It was a perfect place for digging whenever he had a few spare minutes away from the bank—which didn't happen to be right now. He took his pocket watch out of his vest and checked it. Then he dropped it back inside.

"We need to get a move on, Ginger, if I'm going to get some work done at the bank before lunch." With his front paws on the saddle horn, and the leather reins that he used to guide Ginger held securely in his teeth, he clicked his tongue. "Let's go, girl." He turned his head left, and by pulling the reins, he turned Ginger left, too.

Ginger trotted under the hanging BAR CIRCLE RANCH sign that had Long Bill's paw print on it. Then the pair headed up the rutted trail toward town.

Long Bill pushed his black nose into the

Vivian Sathre

breeze and sniffed. "Do you smell that, Ginger? Fresh Texas air. Isn't it wonderful? You don't get air like that inside a stuffy bank."

At that moment Ginger stopped and lifted her tail. Long Bill looked at the ground behind her and pawed his nose. "Or that."

When Ginger started to walk again, Long Bill nudged the brim of his derby with his front paw.

"Yessiree, Bob. I'd trade this fancy hat and my paper-pushing bank duties for a good old Stetson cowboy hat and the wide open range any day."

Careful not to drop the reins, he licked his lips.

"Freedom—I can almost taste it. On the range a man can live by his own code—friendship, honor, and trust mean everything. Not like at the bank, where things have to be done in a strict, follow-all-the-rules, back-east big-city way." A train whistle blew in the distance. "How about you, Ginger—don't you miss the good old days?"

When Ginger didn't answer, Long Bill sighed.

"You don't listen to a word I say, do you?"

A gust of wind herded a family of tumbleweeds across the trail in front of him. It reminded Long Bill of his days of herding cattle.

"I sure do miss being out on the range. Tom

30

Merwin and I made a great team. I couldn't ask for a better trail hand to work with or a better friend." Long Bill adjusted the reins in his mouth. "The two of us were an independent breed—no one bossed us around. Why, there wasn't an obedience school in all the land that could tame us!"

Ginger ignored him.

As they continued toward town, the memory of one particular trail ride stuck in Long Bill's head like fleas to a pup. . . .

I was taking a few hundred head of cattle to Kansas. My trail hands were riding up ahead, keeping the herd on course. Except for Tom. He and I were what was called drag riders. We rode behind the herd, rounding up stragglers, pushing them toward the drove. Actually, Tom rode on horseback, but most of the time I chose to be on my own four feet. Following the herd like that, we swallowed a lot of dust. Even a neckerchief pulled over my muzzle didn't help much. Luckily, I didn't mind the taste of dirt, and I actually liked the smell of it.

"Yeah. Yeah! Get along, little dogie," I called. I ran like the wind behind a calf, my chaps protecting my hind legs as I got too near some sagebrush. "Yee-haw, yeah!" I drove the

calf back toward the herd. On the other side, Tom guided a cow in. When he did, the calf shot off again, refusing to join the pack. Barking, I raced up and stopped him from getting away from the herd. The calf ran back toward Tom, still trying for its freedom. The two of us kept that calf zigzagging all the way to camp. He was one tuckered-out little feller by nightfall.

Of course, so was I. And all that running had made my paws burn as if they'd just been branded. I sighed with relief as I joined Tom on a grassy mound near the campfire. He sat with his back to the flames, our gear next to him. As usual, without even being asked, he was keeping an eye on the herd.

I sniffed around a bit. Then I sat down next to him with my back to the fire, too. As I stared out at the cattle below, my fur soaked up the heat from the flames.

Finally, I dug my harmonica out of my pocket. "Any special requests, Tom?"

Smiling, Tom looked over at me. "Are you still playing songs so sad you make even the orneriest critters cry tears the size of potatoes?" He leaned away, then tossed me my bedroll.

"I am," I said. I opened my roll with my nose. A stranger might have thought we were *about to argue, but Tom and I had been best friends for a long time. We knew each of us was only funnin' the other.*

Behind us, on the other side of the campfire, sat Calliope Catesby. He was near the chuck wagon; he and some of the other trail hands were gambling.

Suddenly, Calliope let out a hoot and a holler that made my fur stand on end. He had been losing money all night. "A full house—I finally got a winning hand, boys!" Calliope took a swig from the jug they were passing around. Then scraping his winnings toward him, he leaned back against the chuck wagon wheel and laughed.

Calliope was a lot like barbed wire; he wasn't much fun to run into, day or night. He'd gambled away every silver dollar he ever got. So he was left with nothing but a hole in his pocket. I tried to think of something nice about Calliope, but when I did, my head emptied out like a barrel of bones with the bottom cut out. Then I remembered a time on the trail when he almost shared his last drink of water with me.

Leaning toward Tom, I lowered my voice so no one else would hear. "It's been a while since Calliope has been in one of his bad humors."

Tom nodded and stole a glance over his shoulder as he tossed another cow chip on the fire. "That's the truth, Bill, sure as shootin'. Calliope has been mighty calm these days. But if he keeps drinking and losing money the way he has been tonight, I don't know how long it's gonna last."

I took a breath, picked up the harmonica in my lips, and began to play softly.

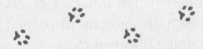

Ginger snorted and jerked her head. Long Bill's mind returned to the present, back to his ride toward town. Long Bill sighed as his memories

35

faded. "Those were the days. . . . It's too bad the cattle boom didn't catch Tom in a stampede of dollars, too. Then again, he still gets to be a cowboy," Long Bill said enviously. "He's an honest man, a hard worker, and a true friend—someone I can always depend on. If that's not success, I don't know what is. All the money in the world couldn't buy those things."

Reaching the white picket fences at the edge of town, Long Bill clicked his tongue and trotted Ginger up Main Street. Raised, wooden board-walks lined both sides of the dirt street. Stores and businesses, built in two long rows, stood along each walk.

Long Bill rode up behind a small herd of cattle being driven through town. "Ya! Ya! Yee-haw!" Long Bill raised a paw to hurry them on. Then he waved to George, a shopkeeper, as he passed him.

Continuing up Main Street, Long Bill stopped Ginger in front of The First National Bank of Chaparosa. The front of the bank was painted light green, and it had a darker green trim. Long Bill had chosen the greens himself. He'd hoped they would make him feel closer to a good ol' roll in the range grass. He sighed. It hadn't worked.

With a dismount to one of the water barrels that was placed around town in case of a fire, Long

Bill tossed the reins around the hitching rail. Then he jumped down to the wooden boardwalk. Before entering the bank, he dusted off his derby and banker's clothes.

Standing on his hind legs and pushing with both front paws, Long Bill opened the door to the bank. Three people stood in line, waiting their turns for service. Before he could stop himself, Long Bill barked at the heels of the undertaker, who was standing too far back in line.

The undertaker jumped ahead, closing the gap between himself and the person in front of him. With a hand over his heart, he turned and looked at Long Bill. "Why, you nearly scared me to death!"

"Sorry." Long Bill lowered his head. "I guess herding is in my blood."

Then he trotted quietly past the customers and went back to his private office. He climbed into his chair, looked at his desk, and groaned.

"Paperwork everywhere." He stretched his neck higher. "Why, the piles are so high I can barely see over them. I sure am glad Tom insists on coming to town every day for lunch. At least I have something to look forward to."

He used his nose to nudge some letters and documents out of the way. Then he opened a ledger book with his paw. The name "Tom Merwin" and the amount of $10,000.00 popped out from the page at him. The loan was made with the understanding that it would be paid back on demand any time—a *call* loan. It was a lot of money to loan someone who didn't have property the bank could take in case he was unable to repay the big loan. But, heck, Long Bill knew Tom and his brother, Ed, were good for it. They had borrowed money to buy cattle. It was a deal they just could not pass up. Ed took the cattle to Kansas City to sell for a profit.

Long Bill stared into the air. The problem was, the loan didn't exactly fit into the banking laws made by those business fellows back east. If that examiner fellow came to town before Ed got back with the cash . . . Well, Long Bill didn't even want to *think* about what would happen.

Long Bill dug around on his desk with his paw. "Now, where's the letter from that doggone bank examiner? If I'm not mistaken, he should be arriving sometime within the week." Sighing, he gave up the hunt. He took off his suit jacket and set to work on the rest of his ledger.

Before Long Bill knew it, two hours had passed. Tom Merwin was standing in the doorway, smiling at him. He wore his usual clothes—

cowboy hat, neckerchief, jeans, and a leather vest over a flannel shirt.

"Happy days, Bill." Tom flipped a coin in the air.

"How are you doing, Tom?" Long Bill wagged his tail, then scratched at a flea homesteading near his ear.

"I'm feeling mighty lucky." Without bothering to remove his hat, Tom crossed the room and sat in a chair near Long Bill's desk.

"Well, I wish I were." Long Bill suddenly spotted the letter he'd been searching for earlier. It was in plain sight on the corner of his desk. He sighed and nosed it toward Tom. He didn't want to insult Tom by asking him when his brother would return so that Tom could pay back the loan. But letting Tom know there was trouble coming around the bend wouldn't hurt. "Take a look at this."

"It's from Philadelphia," Tom said, eyeing it.

"I received that by Pony Express the other day." Long Bill put a paw on his desk. "That double-magnifying-eyeglass-wearing bank examiner is coming back to Chaparosa! I tell ya, that man could find something bad in the middle of a church."

"Oh, come on, Bill," Tom said, the news not affecting his good mood. "I'm sure your books

are straight as an arrow. You're an honest man, Bill." He leaned closer and held up a shiny silver dollar. "Look at this. I found it across from the livery stable. I'm gonna take it as a good-luck sign. I'm gonna ask her today." The toe of his boot started tapping the floor, as it usually did when he was nervous.

Long Bill wagged his tail. It was clear his friend's mind was not on any loan. "You wouldn't be referring to the lovely Mame Dugan, now, would you?" Long Bill asked.

Mame was so beautiful she could win the Best of Breed in any show. But Long Bill's instincts told him Mame wasn't interested in being courted for marriage by any man. And so far, Long Bill's instincts had never been wrong.

"The one and only." Tom looked as happy as a bedbug in a boardinghouse. He stood. "Care to come along and see how it's done?"

Long Bill jumped down from his chair and gave his back legs a stretch. "You saved me from a mound of paperwork, Tom. I guess it's only fitting I save you from a broken heart when Mame turns you down flat," he teased.

Tom tossed the silver dollar in the air and chuckled. "Not today, Bill. Today's my lucky day. Just you wait and see!"

Wishbone's Wild West Word Bank

Howdy! It's me, Wishbone. I reckon some of the words and phrases in this book are a mite unfamiliar to you. I've rounded up some of these pesky rascals and created my own dictionary.

as confused as a hibernatin' rattler wakin' up in a snowstorm   rattlesnakes hibernate during the cold-weather season and wake up when the weather warms up. Now, if one of those fellows woke up while it was still snowing, he wouldn't know what to do!

bank examiner   the man in charge of checking through the bank's record books to make sure the people who work for the bank are following the rules

baron of beef and bone   a dog's way of describing a person of power in the cattle business

bedroll   bedding rolled up for carrying

boardinghouse   a public house where a number of people rent rooms on a day-by-day basis, and where meals are provided by the owner

call loan   a loan made with the agreement that when the lender wants his money back, all he has to do is *call in* the loan, and the money has to be repaid immediately

cattle boom   rapid, widespread growth of the cattle business

cattle chip   dried manure that is thrown on a fire and burned instead of wood

chaps   seatless pants, made of strong leather, worn over regular pants

chuck wagon   the wagon that carries and serves food out on the trail

cowpoke   cowboy

cud-chewing critter   a cow or similar animal that brings up a mouthful of food from its stomach for a slow, second chewing in the mouth

dadgum   darn

derby   a man's stiff felt hat with a dome-shaped top and a narrow brim that runs all around

dogie   a motherless calf in a herd on the range

done by the book   done according to the rules

don't cotton to the idea   don't like the idea

drove   a group of animals that moves as a single unit

dry goods   cloth or clothing, and other small, useful items like pins and thread

full as a beehive at sundown   feeling very full after eating a big meal (bees are back in their hive by sundown)

gather that feller in   capture him

greenbacks paper money

happy as a bedbug in a boardinghouse   very happy (a boardinghouse has lots of old, lumpy mattresses for bugs to live in)

he looks like he just stepped off a catalog page   dressed perfectly from head to toe

highfalutin   stuck-up

homesteading near his ear   living near his ear (like a flea)

hot under the collar   really, really angry

ornery   unfriendly, grouchy, and bad-tempered

powerful   a large amount of; great

put on the dog   to look and act one's best to impress someone

reach the end of his rope   He can't take it anymore.

reckon   think; guess

reins   leather straps fastened to each side of a bit (a bit is worn in a horse's mouth). They are used to control the animal, and to indicate to the animal which way it should turn. Reins are like the steering wheel on a horse.

saddlebag   a large pouch with a flap that is carried hanging from a saddle. It is used to carry things.

saddle horn   the knob on the front of a western-style saddle

skitter   run away

stampede of dollars   a wild rush of money

steed   horse

Stetson   a cowboy hat with a broad brim and a high top

stand there like a tree stump   do nothing

trail hand   a cowboy hired to herd cattle from one place to another, usually to sell them

turn up his toes   to be shot down (land on his back, his toes pointing toward the sky)

you can teach an old dog new tricks   Even though someone has behaved one way for a long time, he can still learn to act differently.

wearin' yer boots   be in your situation; be in your place

with a different roll of the dice   if someone's luck had been different

work honest and sleep sweet   If you're honest, you don't have a guilty conscience to keep you awake at night.

Chapter Three

After trotting out the bank door and onto the wooden boardwalk, Long Bill paused and looked at Tom. "What do you say we ask Marshal Buck to come along for lunch?"

"Sounds good," Tom said, following his friend out into the sunlight.

Long Bill watched a wagon roll by and throw up dust. As he made his way up the raised boardwalk, riders on horseback passed him, waving as they went. All up and down the boardwalk, people were strolling and chattering, enjoying the sunshine.

Long Bill nodded greetings to the folks as he passed. "It sure feels good to be out of that bank," he said to Tom.

Tom drew in a deep breath and smiled. "It's a fine day, isn't it, Bill?"

"Reckon you said something we can finally agree on, Tom." Long Bill wagged his tail, then studied his friend. "That's quite a bounce you have to your step today—almost as if you're walking on air."

Laughing, Tom flipped his silver dollar.

Watching the coin drop back into Tom's hand, Long Bill again thought about the letter from the Philadelphia bank examiner. "Say, have you heard from your brother Ed lately?" he asked, casual-like.

Tom shook his head. "No. Not yet. But he'll be along. Don't you worry."

"I s'pose you're right," Long Bill said, hoping it was so. He stopped and raised a paw to greet Miss Wilhemina, who was leaving George's store. "Good day to you, Miss Wilhemina."

She smiled, then continued on. The hem of her long skirt brushed across Long Bill's furred feet. Coming out the door behind her was George. A crisp, white apron covered his clothes. On his shoulder he was carrying two sacks of flour. He set them on top of a stack he'd already started and tipped his hat. "How are things at the bank, Bill?"

"Can't complain," Long Bill said pleasantly, wagging his tail. "Can't complain."

Tom and George exchanged brief greetings. Then Tom and Long Bill walked on.

Tom stepped up his pace.

Whoo-ee! He must really be eager to talk to Mame, Long Bill thought. He smiled to himself and pumped his four legs faster.

As they neared the end of the street, the boardwalk cleared. Long Bill caught sight of the marshal lounging in a wooden rocking chair on the walk in front of his office. He was reading a newspaper.

Long Bill quickly trotted over to the marshal and sat by his feet. The marshal was wearing black work boots that covered his pants legs to just below the knees.

"How do, Buck?" Long Bill said. "Would you care to join us over to Mame's for lunch?"

Sighing, Marshal Buck folded up his newspaper and set it aside. "No, not today, Bill. I'm glad to see you, though." He reached out to shake hands with Tom. "Nice to see you, Tom." His coat gaped open, giving a full view of the marshal's badge pinned to his tan vest.

"Same here, Buck." Tom nodded.

Long Bill liked the slow, lazy way the marshal talked, but he noticed Tom was getting a bit fidgety. "What can I do for you, Buck?" Long Bill asked.

"I'll go over an' get us some stools, Bill," Tom

said, wriggling around as if he had ants in his boots. "See ya, Buck." With a wave, he started out in the direction of Mame Dugan's Restaurant.

Buck pushed his hat back a bit and nodded across the street.

Long Bill followed Buck's gaze. He saw big, burly Calliope Catesby, his face sweaty and smudged with dirt. He was huffing and puffing as he loaded sacks of cattle feed onto a freight wagon.

"Calliope's been putting out signals of an approaching bad mood again. He's been finding fault with everything that's said to him." Buck paused to rock slowly. "Sam the bartender said lately Calliope's been drinking more and keeping him busier than a beaver building a double-decker dam. And this morning I saw him kick his own dog off the porch of the hotel—and he refused to apologize!"

A shiver willy-nillied its way from the tip of Long Bill's nose to the tip of his tail. "No apology? Well, that is a bad sign, indeed." As Long Bill looked on, Calliope removed his hat and wiped his forearm across his sweaty forehead.

Buck's chair squeaked as he rocked a bit faster. "Could be he's about to go off on another shooting spree."

Careful to keep his tail out from under the

rocker, Long Bill put a paw on the chair. "Well, Buck, I suppose the best thing to do is to keep an eye on him, as you've been doing. And don't you worry, I'll be here to help you if you need me."

Nodding slowly, the marshal picked up his newspaper and opened it. "Thanks, Bill. And I'll take you up another day on that lunch invitation."

Long Bill trotted down the stairs leading off the raised wooden boardwalk. Putting his nose to the ground, he sniffed around the dirt for a bit. He didn't pick up any interesting scents. So, when the street was clear of rolling wagons and hurrying horses, he crossed. He headed toward the inviting yellow building with orange trim—Mame Dugan's Restaurant.

A man wearing a highfalutin three-piece suit came out of the train station and walked down the stairs. He looked clean and crisp, as if he had just stepped off the page of a clothing catalog. Carrying a black briefcase at his side, the man walked stiffly toward Long Bill.

I'd say this is the only other fellow in town besides me who doesn't have a Colt .45 strapped to his side, Long Bill thought. As the man got close enough for careful inspection, Long Bill cringed inwardly. *It's that double-magnifying-eyeglass-wearing bank examiner from back east.*

The man tipped his expensive black derby. "Mr. Longley, do you remember me? J. Edgar Todd, bank examiner."

Nodding, Long Bill hesitantly offered him his paw. "I wasn't expecting you for another day or so, Mr. Todd."

The man accepted Long Bill's offer. After a quick shake, however, he pulled a linen handkerchief from his pocket and wiped off his fingers.

Paw-leezz! Long Bill thought. *A little bit of dirt never hurt anybody. In fact, it usually makes me feel much better. Something tells me this guy's never tried rolling in it after a bath!*

J. Edgar Todd eyed him. "Ah, Mr. Longley, I imagine we work a bit faster and more productively back east than you people here do out west. I've come all the way from Philadelphia to examine your books."

Long Bill swallowed down a growl and forced himself to wag his tail. "Well, Mr. Todd, you'll find the First National Bank just down the way on your right. Ask anyone for help. I'll be at Mame Dugan's Restaurant, directly across the street." He nodded.

"Very good, sir." J. Edgar Todd tried to turn and go, but something held him back.

With his keen hearing, Long Bill heard a

faint squishing sound. Looking down at Mr.
Todd's feet, he held back a chuckle. The man was
standing in a pile of manure.

"Cow pie," Long Bill explained, as Mr. Todd
freed one foot. *The closest this city slicker has ever
been to a real cow is probably when he's eaten a bowl
of beef stew.*

Mr. Todd's face turned the color of a fresh-cut
steak. "Uh . . . I shall meet up with you at the
restaurant," he said. After unsuccessfully trying to
stomp the mess from his shoes, he strutted toward
the bank in a proper, efficient manner.

We may not put on the dog out west by dressing up in fancy duds every day, but at least we know where to step, Long Bill thought, thumping his tail. Glimpsing another pile of manure in the middle of the street, he howled with laughter. *Or, rather, where* not *to step!*

Long Bill faced Mame's and broke into a trot. "I hope Tom hasn't tried out his lucky silver dollar yet. I sure don't want to miss all the excitement."

Chapter Four

That Sunday evening Ellen drove her Ford Explorer toward Pepper Pete's Pizza Parlor. Wishbone stretched his neck to stick his nose out a partially opened backseat window. "You should try this," he said to Joe, sitting on the seat beside him. "It's really energizing. All those different smells—my pal Fritz, barbecued ribs, fresh-cut grass . . ." He pulled back. "Here—want to use my window?"

Joe reached over and scratched behind Wishbone's ear.

"Ahh!" Wishbone leaned into his hand. "That's the best 'no' I've ever felt."

"Thank you for driving, Ellen," Wanda said, fidgeting in the front seat. She smoothed the wrinkles from her blue skirt. "I'm so nervous I probably would have been a road hazard."

Ellen smiled. "It's not a problem, Wanda. You've had quite a day."

Wanda chuckled. "I sure have." She turned toward the backseat. "Wishbone, here, has, too."

Wishbone wagged his tail. "All in a day's work for the fearless—and, might I add, *adorable*—terrier. Adorable, *hungry* Jack Russell terrier."

When they reached Pepper Pete's, Wishbone trotted inside eagerly. Wagging his tail, he greeted everyone personally. "Hello, Walter, Melina, Marcus. Hello, Travis. Okay, time to eat."

The group had gotten together at Pepper Pete's to watch the news on TV.

Wishbone looked around. "Hey! Where's the pizza? Ellen, maybe you should have called ahead."

Wishbone sniffed the floor for crumbs. A half-minute later his head popped up.

"Walter, you should fire whoever's in charge of clean-up. The person's much too thorough—there's not a tidbit left anywhere." He sniffed underneath a table near a wall. "Besides, you could hire me to do the job for almost nothing. Let's just say I'd work for crumbs. Ha! Ha-ha! Walter? Walter, you're not listening." Wishbone stared at the group. "Helllooo! Anybody? Feed the dog."

Walter and the others were busy talking to one another—except for Melina. She was sitting in one of the red-upholstered booths, reading.

Wishbone sighed and jumped up beside her. "I love books. They're full of adventure. What are you reading?" He moved so he could better see the front of the book, but the girl's hands covered the title. "Hmm . . ."

Melina turned a page and kept her eyes moving quickly along the lines of words.

Wishbone lay down. "Okay. Tell me later."

Finally, Sam came out from behind the counter with a tray loaded with glasses and three pitchers of ice water. "Hi, Wishbone. Hi, Melina."

Melina glanced up and smiled. "Hi."

"Hi, Sam," Wishbone said, without much enthusiasm.

Sam set the tray down and gave Wishbone a piece of sausage that she had pulled out of her apron.

"For me?" Wishbone took it from her hand and gulped the meat. "Thank you. Thank you. Thank you! Delicious. Is the pizza almost ready?"

Wanda checked her watch. "Okay, everybody." She started herding everyone toward the corner of the pizza parlor where Walter had set up a TV. Putting a hand to her cheek, she eyed their three

tables and tried to coordinate the seating arrangements. "Let's see," she said nervously. "Where are the best places to sit so everyone can see the TV? Travis, Melina . . . Okay, you two sit over there, on that side." She turned around. "Oh, Marcus. Let's see. Here you go." She touched a chair at the center table.

"Okay." Marcus sat.

"Hurry, hurry." Wanda waved her hands to motion to everyone else. "Oh, Ellen! Hmm . . . Ellen, you sit right here, next to Marcus." She smiled and pointed. "Let's see, Joe and Sam, you can sit on that side."

As everyone settled into their assigned seats,

Wishbone joined Joe and Sam. Lying down by Joe's feet, he heard Sam whisper to Joe. "I don't think I've ever seen Miss Gilmore so excited."

"Me, neither," Joe said.

Wanda looked back and forth between two of the tables. "No, no . . . here you go." She touched Marcus and Melina on their shoulders. "You two switch." Satisfied with her latest arrangement, Wanda finally sat down at the table with Ellen and Melina.

"Breadsticks all around," Walter said, armed with several baskets from the kitchen. As he set a basket on each table, he glanced at the TV. "Oh, look, everybody. It's starting!" Pulling the remote control from the pocket of his red-white-and-green apron, he raised the volume of the set. Then he sat down.

"Oh. Oh." Wanda wriggled nervously in her chair and stared at the television. "It's Helen Davidson, the news anchor. And there we are!" She pointed to the shot of her and Melina jumping off the stage.

Wishbone moved his head for a better view of the set. "Gosh, I'm handsome. Look at that nice, strong chin. Oh . . . is that another whisker? Hey, I'm growing up, too, Joe, just like you! Now I can go to high school, too!"

"Oh, Melina," Wanda said. "I thought the news story was going to show more of the glee club."

"That's okay," Melina said.

"Melina's so lucky. She gets to be on television!" Marcus tipped in his chair, lost his balance, and began to fall backward. He reached out just in time and grabbed the table, saving himself and his chair from spilling to the floor.

Travis gave Marcus *a look*.

"Uh-oh, Marcus!" Wishbone whispered. "I get that very same look from Ellen. At our house it means *Don't do that again*."

Helen Davidson, from her desk in the TV studio newsroom, began to report as the picture replayed. "Spectators watched in horror as twelve members of the glee club from Sequoyah Middle School in Oakdale were rescued from being hit by the collapsing stage lights by Wanda Gilmore and her dog, Wishbone."

Wishbone bolted up to all fours in alarm. "*Her* dog! And they call themselves a news program? Somebody set that woman straight."

Helen Davidson continued. "Reporter Mitch McCain was on the scene when the accident happened."

The picture switched back to Oak Street and the carnival. Melina was sitting where she'd landed in the sand in front of the stage. She was rubbing her foot. Beside her, Wanda was sitting, holding her wrist. Suddenly the camera zoomed in on a surprised-looking Wanda.

The reporter held out his mike. "Wanda, how did you know the accident was going to happen?"

"Well, I didn't," the television Wanda said. "I didn't, but Wishbone, here, did, and it was all because of him that I was able to get to Melina in time. . . ."

The camera panned to Wishbone, then moved to scan the crowd around them.

The picture changed again, back to Helen Davidson, in the newsroom. "Wanda Gilmore, owner and operator of the town's newspaper, *The Oakdale Chronicle,* is not only one of Oakdale's leading citizens, but its newest local hero. In an upcoming report, we'll be profiling the life and times of Wanda and her amazing dog, Wishbone."

Cheers went up from the group at Pepper Pete's.

Wanda laughed.

"Oh, Wanda, how exciting!" Ellen said.

"Isn't that something!" Wanda had a dreamy look on her face as Walter turned off the set.

"I'll say." Wishbone moved right up and stared at the darkened television screen. "I look twice as big on TV. Don't you agree, Wanda? . . . Wanda?" Wishbone turned around.

Wanda, with a hand resting against her throat, was staring off into space, smiling.

Wishbone lowered his voice. "Earth to Wanda. Come in, Wanda." Wishbone walked back and forth in front of the set. "Helllooo!"

Joe grinned. "Wishbone just loves all this attention."

"Yes, he does!" Wishbone agreed. "He also loves pizza."

Wanda looked at Joe. "I'm sorry they think Wishbone is *my* dog."

"How do you think *I* feel?" Wishbone asked. "But we did make a pretty good team."

"It's okay." Joe shrugged. "It's fun seeing him on TV."

"They asked if he could be there for my profile." Wanda raised her eyebrows. "Is that okay?"

Joe nodded. "Sure."

"Uh . . . Joe?" Wishbone wagged his tail nervously. "Maybe you should come, too. Remember, Wanda's an inexperienced dog lover." He watched Wanda take a bite of breadstick.

"I think Wishbone's trying to get your attention, Miss Gilmore," Joe said.

"Bingo!" Wishbone wagged his tail. "We have a winner.

Wanda looked over at Wishbone.

"Okay, and since no one's noticed, I'll tell you right out—I'm starving!" Wishbone neared Wanda's chair. "Drastic conditions call for drastic measures." He sat up and begged, resting his front paws on the red-and-white-checked tablecloth that hung down from the table. "Whew! All this publicity is giving me quite an appetite. What about you, Wanda?"

"Okay, here you go, Wishbone." Wanda tore off a piece of soft breadstick and held it out. Wishbone opened his mouth and took the piece from Wanda.

Wishbone chewed. "Oh, oh, mmm-mmm. Garlic. Thank you, Wanda." Bread crumbs dropped out of his mouth. "Eating is such a civilized activity." Then he bent down and licked up the crumbs that had fallen on the floor.

Marcus leaned toward Wanda. "Miss Gilmore, what's a 'profile'?"

Wanda's face lit up. "That means the station is going to do a brief story of my life—you know, bits and pieces. Just the highlights—the really interesting stuff."

Marcus's eyes opened wide. "Hey, that's really neat."

"It is, isn't it?" Wanda agreed.

As Ellen excused herself from the table, Wanda turned to Melina, a bit puzzled. "I'm not sure why Mitch McCain is focusing so much on me. After all, this is your story, too. Why don't you come down to the *Chronicle* with me tomorrow?" She smiled. "Maybe we can get Mr. McCain to cover the next glee club performance."

Melina shook her head. "No, thanks, anyway, Miss Gilmore."

The smile on Wanda's face was replaced by a look of concern. "Melina, you aren't embarrassed, are you? There's no need to be embarrassed one little bit. . . ."

Melina shook her head and smoothed the dog-eared corner of her book. "It's just that . . . sometimes I get funny feelings about certain people." Melina sighed. "I don't know. Sometimes they're not even right. But I'm just not sure about Mr. McCain."

"Me, neither!" Wishbone put a paw on the booth seat. "He grabbed my leash as if he owned me!"

Relaxing a bit, Wanda smiled. "Well, if you change your mind, come over to my office tomorrow—"

"I'd go if it were me!" Marcus interrupted excitedly. "I think it'd be cool having a reporter do a story about my life."

"I'm sure you would, Marcus." Wanda smiled at him, then turned back to Melina. "You could be right about Mitch, but . . . well . . ." Wanda thought for a while. "I've never had anyone interested in doing a story about my life before. And he seems sincere. He even called me a *hero*." She reached out and touched Melina's arm. "Are you sure you won't change your mind?"

Melina shook her head.

"You know, Wanda," Wishbone said, "it's wise for Melina to trust her own instincts. Ask any dog—they'll all tell you the same thing. Now, my instincts tell me that if I stand up and take that last breadstick off the table, you might get upset." Wishbone stepped closer and wagged his tail.

"But you know what? I'm starved—" Wishbone stretched up and snatched the breadstick in his teeth.

"Wishbone!" Wanda and Melina scolded in unison.

Wishbone gulped down the evidence. "What? Somebody talking to me?"

As Wishbone trotted off to friendlier territory, he thought about Long Bill Longley making his way across the dusty street to Mame Dugan's Restaurant. *That lucky dog can order anything he wants to eat. . . .*

Chapter Five

Long Bill dodged a tumbleweed rolling down the street and trotted toward the sound of the piano music. It was coming from Mame Dugan's Restaurant. Mame's was the most popular place to eat in Chaparosa. If any place could be called the center of town, it was Mame's. And Long Bill made sure he never missed a meal!

Long Bill climbed the steps to the boardwalk, then walked under the swinging doors that led into the restaurant. He stopped and sniffed. *Mmm-mmm. The smells coming from that kitchen are enough to set my black nose a-twitching.*

He looked toward the corner to the chalkboard Mame kept on an easel. He tried to read the list of "Today's Specials" written on the board, but there were too many cowboys in the way. Just like every other day at high noon, the restaurant was packed with dusty cowboys who'd put down their work to pick up a fork.

"Howdy, Bill!" The men all turned to Bill and called in unison.

"Howdy, everyone," Bill replied. He looked from table to table as the men stuffed their mouths full. Sure as shootin', these cowboys had the worst table manners west of the Mississippi.

Okay, he thought, *so most of them are using silverware. But they chew with their mouths open and get food caked in their whiskers. They also slurp, pick their teeth with a fork, and burp louder than a longhorn moose.* Long Bill wagged his tail. *In other words— they eat just like me! I love it! This is my kind of place, and these are my kind of people!*

Smiling, Long Bill made his way past George, who sat with a great big cloth napkin tucked into the neck of his shirt, eagerly awaiting his noon time feast.

Suddenly Long Bill stopped in his tracks. His keen hearing detected something hitting the floor. With a slight turn of his head, he spotted it—a wayward piece of biscuit! He scooted under a chair to his right. One gulp and that biscuit was history!

Trotting on to the counter, Long Bill jumped up on a nearby chair, climbed onto the end stool, then walked across the row of stools. He planted his tail on the one next to Tom.

"Did I miss anything?" Long Bill asked Tom, as the piano player in the corner started to play his next number—"Oh, My Darling, Clementine." Long Bill cocked his head and looked closer at his friend. Tom had a worried look on his face. He was wriggling on his stool like a cow jumping over the hot coals of a campfire. "What's wrong, Tom? You look as if you just sat in a big old pile of sage-brush. . . ."

Tom's eyes darted around nervously as he checked and rechecked his pockets. "I lost my lucky silver dollar."

Long Bill put a paw on the counter. "That's too bad, Tom." He wondered what Tom's next move with Mame would be.

Just then Mame Dugan, the lovely young red-haired, dark-eyed owner of the restaurant, pushed her way out of the swinging doors that led from the kitchen. Small pearl earrings dangled from her ears, swaying gently as she rushed off to deliver the plates of food that loaded down her arms. Her long skirt swishing as she went, she nodded to Tom and Long Bill in passing. "I'll be right with you, boys."

Judging by the look on his face, Tom seemed

to calm down a bit, but his foot started wriggling. "Know why I like her, Bill?"

"Hmm . . . Because she's a good cook?" Long Bill asked, his hind paw digging at a flea on his neck.

Tom shook his head and let his glance follow Mame around the room. The corners of his mouth turned up just a bit. "It's 'cause she's so full of life and self-confidence." He lowered his voice as Mame worked her way back toward them. "She's tough, Bill, *and* beautiful."

Fine qualities, Bill thought. *If she had two more legs and a tail, I might be sweet on her myself.* "Mame has always looked life straight in the eye. . . ." Long Bill's words trailed off as Mame delivered the last plate of food and then came over to the counter.

She looked at Tom with a tired gaze in her eyes. "Now, what can I get ya, honey?"

Tom shifted in his seat but didn't say a word. He just kept staring across at Mame with his big brown eyes. He looked as if he were a pup waiting to be picked from the litter and taken home.

Long Bill cocked his head and looked at his friend. *An arrow from Cupid sure can make a fellow act powerfully funny,* he thought. *I'd better see if I can bring him around before Mame gets to thinking his head has been hollowed out like a pumpkin.*

He placed a paw on the counter. "What's the matter, Tom—cat got your tongue?" he joked. When Tom didn't respond, Long Bill drew Mame's attention to himself. "Well, I think I'll have the meat loaf with mashed potatoes and gravy, fried chicken and black-eyed peas, turkey potpie, and a big ole steak smothered in onions. I'm eating on the light side today. That banker's got me a mite nervous."

"Is that all you want to eat?" Mame raised her eyebrows. "We're also running a special on lamb stew, you know."

Oh, boy! Long Bill got so excited he wagged his tail. "Bring it on, Mame. And could you throw

71

in half a dozen biscuits? I've always been mighty partial to biscuits. They remind me of my trail-riding days."

"Sure, Bill," Mame said with a nod. Then she turned toward Tom, a bit impatient. "Now, what about you?"

"Uh . . . I'll just have the same as Bill," he mumbled.

Mame Dugan shook her head, smiling. "Are you sure that's going to be enough for a big, strong man like you, Tom?"

Well, that did it for Tom. His face lit up like one of those gas lamps used in the cities to light the streets at night. He sat taller and puffed out his chest.

As Mame disappeared into the kitchen, Tom turned to Long Bill and grinned from ear to ear. "Did you hear that? She thinks I'm strong! And did you see the way she smiled at me, Bill? Shucks! I reckon I'll go forward with my plan—even without my lucky dollar."

When the swinging doors behind them squeaked open and *swooshed* shut, Tom and Long Bill turned and looked. Standing just inside the doorway was the unshaven, scruffy, ill-mannered Calliope Catesby.

The fur on Long Bill's neck bristled. He sensed

just by looking at Calliope that the man was about to be as kind as a cat with his claws out.

Sizing up the place, Calliope made his way through the noonday diners. He slowed down behind George, the owner of the general store. He gave George a couple of hefty pats on the shoulder. "Well, well, if it isn't our local seller of goods both fine and general," he said in a sarcastic voice.

Watch it, George, Long Bill thought as he looked on. *Calliope's hoping to find someone to pick a bone with.*

When George ignored Calliope, the cowpoke moved on to Daniel Lawson, a cowboy stuffing his face with Mame's biscuits and gravy. Every time he shoved a big piece in, a bunch of little pieces fell out.

Long Bill wanted to leap down and lap the crumbs off the floor, but he decided to squash his hunger pangs until his main courses arrived.

Calliope held out a hand to point at Daniel. "And here is a living example of local knowledge and fine social manners. Your mother must be very proud." He sneered, showing his crooked teeth, then stepped toward the counter.

Long Bill exchanged glances with Tom as Calliope walked closer.

With a *whump!,* Calliope sat on the stool

next to Long Bill. He gave a slight nod. "Bill." He hadn't washed in a few days. His teeth were yellow and his hat was dirty. And his vest and neckerchief were sweat-stained.

Long Bill knew Calliope was forcing himself to be polite. He sensed a restlessness about the man. With one quick wag of his tail, Long Bill returned the greeting. "Hello, Calliope."

Then, without a hint of a smile between them, Tom and Calliope exchanged nods.

Just then Mame returned from the kitchen and Calliope gave her his full attention. "Well, howdy, Mame."

"Howdy, Calliope. What can I get you?" She poured coffee for him and Tom.

When Long Bill nudged his cup with his nose, Mame grabbed a jug from the counter behind her. She poured Long Bill some water. No caffeine for Long Bill—it would prevent him from taking his mid-afternoon snoozes.

Smiling, Calliope turned on the charm. "I know whatever you have is the best there is, Mame. I reckon I'll just have the usual."

Mame spun on her heels. "I'll be back before your stomach growls," she said, breezing toward the kitchen.

When one of the cowboys at a table behind

them let out a burp loud enough to rattle the windows, Calliope turned and scowled.

Quickly, Long Bill tried to divert Calliope's attention and ward off trouble. "So, Calliope, I saw you loading sacks of cattle feed onto a freight wagon earlier."

"Yeah?" Calliope pushed up his sleeves. "And I s'pose you wanna make somethin' of it?"

So much for my idea of trying to keep Calliope from losing his temper, Long Bill thought. He licked his whiskers. "You're barking up the wrong tree, Calliope. I was just making polite conversation, that's all."

"Well," Calliope said, picking up his cup and squinting at Long Bill, "I don't need you rubbin' my nose in the difference between our financial situations."

Tom twisted on his stool. "For cryin' out loud, Calliope, nobody's rubbin' your nose in nothin'. Nobody cares a hoot about your money matters—"

Mame backed her way through the kitchen doors, turned, then set heaping plates down before Tom, Long Bill, and Calliope. "This'll get you boys started." As she refilled their cups, Tom and Calliope tucked cloth napkins into their shirt collars.

Long Bill thought about tucking a napkin into his collar. *Nah,* he decided.

Tom smiled his thanks to Mame, while Long Bill dug into the mashed potatoes and gravy. "Mmm-mmm." He licked his lips and his nose so he wouldn't waste a drop.

"Thank you kindly, Mame." Calliope was talking pecan-pie-sweet again. "Mame? I wonder if you'd do me the honor of joining me on a sunset ride this evenin'." He slurped his hot coffee. A shower of dribbles fell from his lips to his plate.

Hmm . . . Long Bill stared over his furred shoulder at Calliope. *The way he's slobberin', it looks as if he has bulldog blood runnin' through his veins.*

Calliope didn't bother to wipe his face. He

just kept right on talking to Mame. "Well, I reckon you'll never see such a sunset as the one you'll see from sittin' atop my trusty steed, Apricot."

Tom had stopped in mid-chew, his mouth closed. He was glaring at Calliope.

Long Bill kept right on lapping up food.

With a sigh and a forced smile, Mame finally spoke. "Calliope, I like you as well as I like any of them fellers around here, but there isn't a man in the world I'd ever spend time with, and there never will be."

Long Bill said, "Maybe you just haven't met the right fellow yet, Mame."

"Do you know what a man is in my eyes?" Mame glared from Long Bill to Calliope, then looked at Tom.

Tom shook his head slowly.

Poor Tom, Long Bill thought. *He looks as confused as a hibernatin' rattler wakin' up in a snowstorm.*

"He's a tomb." Mame planted her hands firmly on her hips. "He's a big hollow chamber just waitin' to fill himself up with beefsteakporkchops-liverandonionsbaconhamandeggs. He's that—and nothin' more." She shook her head in irritation. "For two years I've watched men eat, eat, eat.

Now they represent nothin' on earth to me but two-legged, cud-chewin' critters."

Long Bill wagged his tail. *Sounds like my kind of folks! It also sounds as if someone got up on the wrong side of the bedroll.*

Calliope shoved half of a biscuit into his mouth. "Well, a man's got to eat, don't he?"

A look of disgust bloomed on Mame's face as she watched Calliope run his food-covered tongue across his ugly teeth. "A man, a sausage grinder, and a sack of flour awaken in me exactly the same feelings."

Calliope frowned. "But, Mame—"

"No, Calliope." She cut him off. "I'll spend time with no man and see him sit at the breakfast table and eat"—her voice rose—"and come back to lunch and eat, and stomp in again at supper to eat, eat, eat!"

"I knew there was some reason I was never interested in Mame," Long Bill muttered, lapping up the last of his steak. *But poor Tom,* he thought, glancing at the bewildered look on his friend's face.

Chapter Six

From his stool in Mame Dugan's Restaurant, Long Bill sensed that Tom was about to say something about Mame calling men "cud-chewin' critters."

Tom cleared his throat and spoke quietlike. "But, Mame, don't girls ever—"

"No, they don't!" Mame planted her hands on the edge of the counter and fixed her glare on Tom. "Girls eat politely. They nibble a little bit. And they use real manners!"

The corners of Tom's mouth turned up a bit and his eyes brightened. "But I thought when you put sweets in front of a girl—"

"For goodness sake, Tom!" Mame interrupted. "Change the subject." She spun around and stormed into the kitchen.

Tom jumped off his stool, whipped the napkin from his collar, and glared at Calliope. His face turned the same shade of red as his neckerchief. "Look at you, Calliope—ain't no woman ever gonna be interested in you no-how! And now you've gone and made Mame jump to conclusions about all men!"

Calliope rose from his stool and faced Tom with fire in his eyes. "Them's fightin' words, Tom!"

Uh-oh. With all the snarlin' and growlin' that are going' on, it looks as if there's gonna be a fight. Long Bill jumped up onto the counter and braced himself on all fours. "Now, hold on a minute, men. There's no sense in fighting over a woman when we got all this good food sitting here getting cold." He nudged Tom's plate with his nose.

But Tom's eyes were locked on to Calliope's. It seemed neither man cared beans about what Long Bill said.

"Helllooo!" Long Bill paced across the counter on all fours.

Tom stood taller and puffed out his chest. "This town ain't big enough for both of us, Calliope."

"I got as much right to live here as you do!" Calliope jutted out his dripping chin. "Just 'cause you got more money than me doesn't mean you can tell me what to do!"

Reaching out with one hand, Tom pushed

Calliope's right shoulder. "Is that a fact?" He scowled.

Calliope stepped closer and returned Tom's push. "Yeah."

"Uh-oh." Long Bill lowered his ears as Tom reached over, yanked the napkin from the neck of Calliope's shirt, and threw it to the floor.

"Oh, yeah?" Tom asked, raising his voice in anger.

"Yeah," Calliope answered back, just as angry.

The two men grabbed each other by their shirtfronts and began to tussle.

"Easy, there, fellas." Long Bill cocked his head as he watched the two men push and pull each other in a circle.

Finally, Calliope planted his feet firmly on the floor. With a grunt and a groan, he picked Tom up and heaved him across the room.

"Hey!"

Tom crashed into Mame's arms just as she stepped from the kitchen carrying platefuls of food. The food, the dishes, and Tom crashed to the floor. Mame glared down at him. Tom dug potatoes out of his neckerchief and pulled himself up to his feet.

"Sorry, Mame."

Fuming, Mame turned away without saying a word. Long Bill caught a glimpse of her face; it was as red as cherry pie. Mame flung open the swinging doors. With a swish of her full skirt, she stomped back into the kitchen.

Across the room, George stood up and stretched his neck for a view of the spilled food. "Hey, that's my meal!" he complained.

Tom frowned at Calliope. "Now look at what you've done."

Calliope pushed back his hat and grinned. "It looks like lunch is on Tom!"

"And I think that puts you *both* in Mame's doghouse," Long Bill barked.

Tom scooped up a big wad of mashed potatoes from a nearby plate and flung it at Calliope. He hit him square in the face.

"I can't see!" Calliope bellowed, turning in a circle.

Immediately, Tom put his boot to Calliope's rear and gave a healthy push, knocking him into George. George went sprawling across a table full of food.

"Hey!" One of the unhappy diners picked up a biscuit and threw it at Tom.

Tom ducked and the biscuit hit another cowboy. Scowling, that cowpoke scooped up a handful of stew and pitched it back. Another cowboy threw a chicken leg and a hunk of apple

pie. Pretty soon every diner in the place—except Long Bill—was throwing food. So many globs of mashed potatoes were sailing through the air that it was beginning to look like an indoor hailstorm.

Long Bill watched the piano player slip down and hide under the piano, while keeping his fingers pressed to the keys to make music.

Long Bill waited until all was clear. Then he stood tall. "Hey, hey, everybody, can't we just talk about this like civilized human—" He dodged a high-flying hunk of meat loaf. "Never mind." Dropping to his belly, he pressed himself to the hard counter.

Mame stormed out of the kitchen, a shotgun in her hands. "That's enough!"

But no one paid any attention to her. She ducked as a round of cheese flew past her ear. Pointing the barrel of the gun upward, Mame fired into the air. *Boom!*

Instantly, the men froze.

Long Bill looked around at the mess. Then he licked a gob of potatoes from the fur on his front leg. "Letting all this good food go to waste is criminal, I tell you. . . ."

All at once, almost every man in the place raced—slipping and sliding—toward the exit. The swinging doors burst open as men, covered from head to toe with food, flew outside to avoid Mame's anger.

Long Bill trotted under the doors and sat on the wooden boardwalk. "No sense in my waitin' around to see if her bite is worse than her bark."

Calliope staggered outside and stumbled past Long Bill. At the edge of the boardwalk, he tripped on the first step and fell down the next two. He bumped smack into . . . J. Edgar Todd.

Oh, no! he's baaack, Long Bill thought, as he watched J. Edgar Todd scowl and move out of Calliope's way.

Calliope lost his balance again. With a splash, he fell into the rectangular trough that the horses drank from. As quickly as he went down, he came bobbing up. Then he climbed out and shook himself off like a dog, spraying water everywhere.

A shocked look came over J. Edgar Todd's face as he stepped back and wiped the water spots from his elegant business suit.

Hey! Calliope is right smart sometimes. Long Bill wagged his tail as he looked at the bank examiner.

As Calliope wandered off, Long Bill turned to Mr. Todd. Before he could speak, the doors to the restaurant flew open again. Tom stepped out, with his hat in hand. Covered with food, he sat down on the top step of the boardwalk and swiped at his face, brushing mashed potatoes from his eyebrows.

Then suddenly the restaurant doors exploded open as if they'd been charged with a stick of dynamite. Mame, a hand on one hip, and a shotgun in her other hand, suddenly stood on the boardwalk. She glared at the men with disgust. "If any of you ever behaves that way again in my establishment," she warned, "well, I'll . . . I'll . . . I'll just have to raise my prices!" She did an about-face, pushed through the doors, and stomped out of sight.

Long Bill noticed a stream of gravy running down the door frame. He went over to it and, with a few quick swipes from his tongue, he made the gravy disappear. "Don't worry, Mame. I'll bring some of my friends by later, and they can lick the place clean." He chuckled. Turning, he faced Mr. Todd.

"Uh . . . my . . . uh . . . My dear Mr. Longley, has there been some sort of trouble?" Mr. Todd peered through his spectacles.

Long Bill sat down next to Tom. "Oh, just another dog day in Chaparosa."

"I see. There's this matter with the books. . . ." J. Edgar Todd tapped the ledger he was carrying under his arm.

"Oh, yes—the books." Long Bill scratched his spotted ear. "Any problems?"

"Well, everything is in order—*except* for a call loan of ten thousand dollars, made to a Mr. Tom Merwin." He held up a finger. "Now, you've violated two national banking laws—"

Long Bill jumped up to all fours. "Now, hold on a cotton-pickin' minute—"

Tipping his head, J. Edgar Todd peered over his glasses at Long Bill and ignored his words. "First, you're not allowed to loan such a large sum of money to one person. Second, you made a loan with no collateral—nothing to hold against the loan—from this Mr. Merwin fellow. Therefore, you have no guarantee the loan will be repaid." Raising his eyebrows, he shook his head slowly. "You're in a very serious position, Mr. Longley. The government has the right to take you to trial for ignoring important banking laws."

"Take me to trial?" Long Bill didn't like the ha-ha-I-gotcha look on J. Edgar's face. "Now, look here just a minute, Mr. Todd. This here's Tom Merwin, right next to me." Long Bill looked at Tom as he started digging mashed potatoes out of his ear.

Tom flung the potatoes from his finger. With a smile, he offered Mr. Todd his hand for shaking. "Howdy."

Eyeing Tom's crusty hand, Mr. Todd shrank back, a disgusted look on his face.

Why, he's looking at Tom as if he's a cow pie, Long Bill growled to himself. "I made that loan to Tom on his word. I have always found that when a man's word is good, it's the best security there is."

Tom nodded. "That's right. My word is as good as a law-abidin', official contract."

Mr. Todd's fingers started tapping impatiently against the ledger he was holding.

"See," Long Bill said, his tail starting to wag, "Tom heard about two thousand head of cattle that could be bought for eight dollars a head."

"Cattle I knew I could sell in Kansas City for

fifteen dollars apiece." Tom continued picking food off himself.

Mr. Todd tipped his hat and grinned. "Be that as it may—"

Long Bill jumped up to a water barrel and sat on his haunches. "His brother, Ed, took the cattle on to market about three weeks ago. He ought to be back any day now with enough money to pay that note—and a whole lot more."

"That's right." Tom gave a quick nod of his head. "That's the plain fact of the matter."

"And I think that makes good business sense, don't you?" Long Bill hoped he'd convinced Mr. Todd to stop acting like a dog with the biggest bone.

J. Edgar Todd glanced at Tom, who still had a powerful amount of food plastered on him, and he grimaced.

Finally, Mr. Todd gave all his attention to Long Bill. "Well, Mr. Longley, I'll tell you what I'm going to do. I'm going to Hilldale tonight to examine a bank there." He took off his glasses. With a cloth he took from his pocket, he wiped the dirt from the lenses. "I'll pass through Chaparosa on my way back home the day after tomorrow. Mr. Longley, you have until noon that day to pay back this loan. Otherwise, I'm afraid I'll have to do my duty." He set his glasses on his nose and hooked the wire stems over his ears. Then, with a tip of his derby, he marched off.

"City slickers." Tom sat there, shaking his head in disbelief.

Long Bill stood up on all fours and shook from nose to tail. "Things sure are done differently back east," he said, wondering how he could solve the problem in less than forty-eight hours.

First, Tom loses his lucky silver dollar. Then he finds out Mame doesn't cotton to being courted. The day isn't turning out at all the way he's expected it would.

Will Wanda's interview with Mitch McCain live up to what she expects? Or does Mr. McCain have a few twists waiting that will send her spinning?

Chapter Seven

Wishbone followed Wanda into the *Chronicle* building Monday morning and past the reception desk. He slowed to look around. The main floor had desks, filing cabinets, and a drafting table. In the back there were two short flights of stairs, one going up and one going down. Following the stairs up took you to Wanda's open office, which looked like a loft and overlooked the main floor. Taking the stairs down would bring you to the archive area, where old newspapers and files were kept. Wishbone knew that the archives had another set of stairs leading down to the basement.

Wishbone sniffed each desk leg he passed. "Definitely a dog-free zone," Wishbone said.

"Oh, look at the cute little dog!"

"Cute, yes. Little, no," Wishbone said, standing tall as he quickly followed Wanda up the stairs and into her office. He crossed the floor and stepped up to the metal railing that formed the outside wall of Wanda's office. It overlooked the entire work area. "Cool. No wall." He stuck his head out through the railing. "Hey! You, down there—*now* who's little?"

He turned around. Against the back wall of Wanda's office was a tree growing in a pot.

Wishbone wagged his tail. "For me, Wanda? How thoughtful."

He turned again to find Wanda checking her hat and hair in a small hand mirror.

"Let me see." Wishbone cocked his head. "Face clean, no burrs in your hair. You look fine."

He perked up his ears and heard the front door open. He went to the rail. It was Mitch McCain. Wishbone tried to catch the conversation between the reporter and one of the *Chronicle* employees. There were so many people down there, including the cameraman, and so much going on, that Wishbone had a hard time hearing them.

"So, what's the atmosphere like here now that you're working with Oakdale's newest hero?" Mitch asked. Then he pushed the mike in the woman's face.

"Yoo-hoo! Up here!" Wishbone wagged his tail. "Ask me! Ask me!"

"Oh, well . . . everybody works very hard here." The woman fidgeted. "But no one works harder than Wanda herself," she quickly added. "Wanda always says if you don't want to work hard, you might be happier somewhere else."

"Maybe I'd better pass that word along to those pink flamingos in Wanda's yard. They just stand around and do nothing all day."

Wishbone watched another employee at a desk nearby motion to the woman for assistance.

"Excuse me." The woman smiled briefly at Mitch McCain, then got up and walked away.

"That's great!" Mitch said to his cameraman.

Wanda joined Wishbone at the railing. When Mitch McCain looked up, she grinned and waved.

"Now, let's move on to Wanda herself," Wishbone heard the reporter say to the cameraman.

Wishbone wagged his tail. "Wanda, they're on their way up here!" He sat tall. "How do I look? I'd better practice my greeting. . . . 'Nice to meet you, Mr. McCain.'" He cleared his throat and lowered his voice. "'Nice to meet you, Mr. McCain.'"

At that moment, Mitch McCain and his cameraman reached the top of the stairway, landing them in a corner of Wanda's office.

Wanda plucked the mirror off her desk and quickly checked her hair again.

"We're going to get some footage of you working," Mr. McCain said to Wanda. "Then we'll get some more sound bites from a few of the other employees."

"Sound bites?" Wanda looked confused as she set down the mirror. "Oh, *sound bites*—record their words. Sounds great! And that reminds me, I made snacks." Smiling proudly, she picked up a plate of cookies from her desk and offered them to Mitch McCain. But he walked past without paying attention to Wanda or the cookies. Wanda's smile collapsed. She set the plate down.

"Hmm . . ." Wishbone cocked his head. "How can you trust someone who'd pass up a cookie?"

Wanda watched Mitch McCain and the

cameraman clear off her desk to set up their equipment for the shoot.

"Helllooo!" Wishbone looked at Wanda. "Testing—one, two, three. Somehow, my voice isn't getting picked up." Footsteps sounded behind him. He looked over his shoulder and saw Samantha at the top of the stairs. With a wag of his tail, he trotted over to greet her. "Hi, Sam!"

Holding the 35mm camera she wore around her neck to keep it from swinging, Sam bent down and ruffled Wishbone's ear.

"Mmm . . . Thanks," he said.

"There you go, Wishbone." Sam patted his side. Then she took a few steps into the office. "Hi, Miss Gilmore."

"Oh, hi, Sam. I'm sorry, but I can't talk to you right now." Smiling, Wanda glanced at Mitch McCain. "The TV people are here."

"I just came to get a few pictures of the interview." Sam held her camera up so Wanda could see it. "Is that okay with you?"

"Oh, of course!" Wanda fiddled with her hat. Then she fingered her dangling star earrings to make sure they were hanging correctly.

Wishbone saw Hank coming up the stairs.

Hank reached the top of the stairs and walked toward Sam. "Hi, Sam. Pretty exciting, huh?"

"Yes!"

Mr. McCain arranged some papers and a pen on Wanda's desk. Then he pulled an orange-plastic chair over from the corner of the room and pointed to it. "Could you just huddle over your desk here, please?" he said abruptly, sinking down into the cushioned leather chair across from her.

"Huddle over here? Well, I usually sit . . . well . . ." Wanda giggled nervously. "Whatever you say, Mr. McCain."

"He's sitting in *her* chair," Hank whispered to Sam as he left, and Wishbone's keen ears caught the remark, too.

I wonder why Mitch McCain doesn't show the scene the way it really is—with Wanda in her real chair, sitting in front of real paperwork, Wishbone thought.

Sitting down, Wanda took the pen in her hand and leaned over the papers as if she were about to write.

"Good. Ready?" Mr. McCain asked.

Wanda nodded.

With a signal from Mr. McCain, the cameraman began to roll the film.

"Hey! What about me?" Wishbone trotted over, stood on his hind legs, and put his front paws on Mitch McCain's legs. "Nice to meet you, Mr. McCain!"

"Wait a minute! Hold the roll," he said impatiently. "Can someone *please* put a leash on the dog?"

"But I'm Wanda's amazing dog, Wishbone." Then he lowered his voice. "I knew the minute this guy passed up a cookie he wasn't trustworthy."

Sam tapped her leg. "Come on, Wishbone."

Wishbone walked away and took a seat on another plastic chair near the railing. "Okay. I'll just . . . wait over here till you're ready for me."

Mitch McCain brushed off his pants legs where Wishbone had put his paws. Then he turned back to Wanda. He held up three fingers. "Okay, in three . . . two . . . one!" He turned to the camera behind him and smiled. "This is Mitch McCain, for Fast News Fifty-seven. Remember, when you're looking for news, look for Mitch McCain. I'm here with Wanda Gilmore, an Oakdale hero, and a woman of mystery, as well."

"Mystery?" Wanda sounded pleasantly surprised.

"This is a very exciting time for you, isn't it, Miss Gilmore?" the reporter asked, sticking his mike right in front of Wanda.

Reaching up, Wanda nervously played with one of her earrings. "Well, yes . . . in a way, I guess it is."

Mitch McCain pulled the mike back to himself. "Miss Gilmore, our investigation has discovered that you not only own *The Oakdale Chronicle* and the beautiful building it's housed in, but you also happen to own the building that Oakdale Sports and Games is in, too. Isn't that so?"

"Watch it, Wanda," Wishbone warned, sitting up alert. "I'm sensing some bad vibes here."

"Well . . . yes, but I've tried to keep that quiet." Wanda considered what she said, then smiled. "Well, I don't mean *'keep'* that quiet." Her hands moved through the air nervously. "It's just that it's rather personal. There are particular reasons for my owning it."

"So you want to keep this a secret for personal reasons." The reporter's tone had taken on a coolness, almost a challenging tone.

This guy is sneakier than a cat! Wishbone thought.

"Wait, wait—please!" Wanda brushed the air with her hands again. "Uh . . . you're twisting my words around," she said, swirling a finger in the air.

"Isn't that what you said?" He prodded her. "There are personal reasons?"

"I wanted to be sure that the old Oakdale firehouse, which is now Oakdale Sports and Games, was preserved." Wanda began to relax. "You see, my father taught me to have a love of the wonderful old buildings in town. So, when I was able to purchase it, I jumped at the opportunity."

"So you began buying up buildings to control the development for . . . your own *personal* reasons," the reporter said accusingly. "I see. Is that also what your father wanted?"

"Helllooo! Maybe you should perk up your ears a little more." Wishbone kept his eyes glued on Mitch McCain. "I've met a lot of poor listeners in my life, but you are the worst!"

"No, of course not." Wanda sat up stiffly. "That is *not* what I meant. You're changing my words again!"

Mitch McCain grinned. "I think I have everything I need." He motioned to the cameraman to stop rolling the film.

Sam and Wanda exchanged puzzled glances. Then they remained there, speechless, while the men quickly packed up their gear. Just before leaving, Mitch grabbed a cookie and stuck it in his mouth. Then he took another one and stuffed it into the pocket of his jacket.

Wishbone jumped off his chair and stood at the top of the stairs, watching the men walk down the stairs. "Thief!" he called. "You don't deserve *any* cookies! Take it from me, buster, you don't get treats when you're bad." Wishbone paced. "Wanda, Sam, do something!"

"Unbelievable!" Sam whispered.

Wanda didn't say a word about what happened. But she looked as sad as a hound dog as she went to the railing and watched the Fast News 57 team talking to the employees below. "Sam, do you think you could take Wishbone home for me?" Her voice had lost its usual enthusiasm. "I really need to get some work done."

Sam checked her watch. "I'd like to, but I have to get back to the pizza parlor to help my dad. It's almost time for the lunch rush to start."

"You could turn me loose, Wanda." Wishbone wagged his tail. "I won't get lost. And I'll go straight home. I promise—unless I meet up with a pal . . . or see a cat along the way. . . ."

"Oh, thank you, anyway, Sam. I'll take him back to Joe later." Wanda sighed and sat down at her desk.

"'Bye, Miss Gilmore." Sam went down the steps.

"'Bye, Sam." Wanda reached over, took a cookie from the plate, then held it out for Wishbone. "Well, boy," she said and sighed again, "I guess it's just you and me."

Wishbone wagged his tail as he chomped through the cookie. "Great cookie. Almond, right? Any oatmeal ones up there?" He licked the crumbs he'd dropped on the floor.

Wanda fed him one more, then started on her paperwork.

"Helllooo!" Wishbone sat up and begged, but Wanda ignored him. "Hmm . . . I guess this means no more treats." He eyed a chair against the wall. "Okay. I'll take a nap."

Wishbone spent the rest of the afternoon snoozing. Then he nosed around down on the main floor of the *Chronicle* when the other employees left for the day.

After a while, he trotted to the row of windows near the front door. Standing on his hind legs, he pushed the curtain aside with his nose and peered outside. "Wanda, it's past my dinner time," he finally said. "Can't we go home now?"

"Wishbone?" Wanda came down the stairs. "Time to go home."

"Thank you for listening."

Wishbone stood still so Wanda could hook his leash on him.

"Nice breeze," he said, stepping outside and sticking his nose in the air. "Hmm . . ." Wishbone looked around. Oak Street looked deserted, but he heard and smelled people.

"Hi, Miss Gilmore." Melina waved from across the street, at the doorway of Oakdale Sports & Games.

Wanda waved back. "Oh, hi. Is your uncle's store still open?"

Wishbone wagged his tail. "Don't forget to say hi to the dog, Melina."

"No." Melina shook her head. "Uncle Travis was on the clean-up committee for the carnival. Marcus and I were helping pick up litter."

"It's really too bad the carnival shut down after only one day." Wanda tilted her head. "I guess the stage accident shook everybody up."

"Come on, Wanda." Wishbone aimed himself left and tugged on the leash. "Dinner-dinner-dinner."

Wanda grabbed her hat to keep it from falling off. Then she pulled Wishbone the other way up the street. "It's such a nice evening, I think we should take the long way home." She waved to Melina, then started strolling up the street.

"Ugh!" Wishbone followed Wanda. "A minute ago you were so good at listening to me. What happened?"

As they approached Snook's Furniture, Wishbone wagged his tail excitedly.

"That's the place with the three televisions," he told Wanda. Wishbone trotted toward the store window. "Wow! Look, Wanda. You're on TV!"

"Oh, my." Wanda smiled as she caught a glimpse of herself. "It's from today's interview." She stared happily at the screens until the picture changed to anchorperson Helen Davidson, in the Fast News 57 newsroom.

"Wanda Gilmore: local hero—or town tyrant?" Helen Davidson asked. "Things may not be as they appear for the Oakdale hero. Learn about her secrets and backroom dealings in Mitch McCain's exclusive investigative report, tomorrow on Fast News Fifty-seven."

"That guy is really, really bad news," Wishbone said, watching Wanda as her mouth dropped open in surprise. He nosed her hand. "Wanda? Wanda, are you okay?"

Chapter Eight

The next afternoon, Wanda paced across the Talbots' living room, hugging one of Ellen's sofa pillows to her stomach. Ellen, Sam, Joe, and Wishbone listened as Wanda told them about the television clip she saw at Snook's the evening before.

"Ellen, I just don't understand it," Wanda said, as she finished her story. "He took everything I said and turned it into something I didn't mean." She threw the pillow down on the sofa and grabbed up another.

Wishbone jumped up to the sofa. "The guy's a human Bruno the Doberman—pure bully all the way."

"It was unbelievable!" Sam said, sitting down next to Wishbone. She picked up Wanda's rejected pillow.

Ellen leaned across the pile of letters and bills

she was working on at the dining room table. She tapped her pen against the table. "Oh, Wanda. You know, I've heard about that guy from Fast News Fifty-seven. He wrecks people's lives just because he wants to get a juicy story."

"But why would he do that to me?" Wanda's eyes opened wide. "He called me a hero."

"Can't we just tell him how great you are?" Sam asked.

"Of course, Wanda. We'll do anything we can to help you," Ellen said.

"Definitely, Miss Gilmore." Joe leaned against the hallway door frame.

Pacing again, Wanda grabbed an apple from the fruit bowl on the dining room table as she went by. She bit into the apple, still hugging the pillow with one arm.

Wishbone's ears perked up at a noise. He cocked his head. "Uh-oh! He's back, Joe! Cover me." Wishbone leaped over the back of the sofa and began to pace. "Okay . . . okay . . . what do we do? I know. Everybody get down here on the floor with me and we'll all duck down real low." He bowed down, then peeked out from behind the sofa.

"I wonder what's wrong with Wishbone," Ellen said.

Joe looked out the window.

Ellen's glance followed Joe's. "It's the TV crew! They are coming here."

"Ohhh! I don't want to talk to that man again." Wanda looked around the room for a place to hide. "I can't face him right now."

"That's okay." Ellen got up and took her neighbor by the shoulders and gently pointed her toward the kitchen. "Why don't you just duck out the back door? We'll handle things."

Holding the pillow up to hide her face from the front windows, Wanda walked across the living room.

Wishbone crawled past the sofa and followed Wanda. "Let's all duck out the back, Ellen!"

It was too late. Joe and Ellen had already reached the front door.

"Oh!" Wanda whispered, hurrying back into the living room to return the pillow to the sofa. She dropped it off and then noticed the apple in her hand.

"Hello?" Joe said, opening the door. The news crew stepped into the front hall just as Wanda replaced the apple in the fruit bowl and sneaked out the back way.

Wishbone wasn't so lucky. "I'm trapped!" He flattened himself to the floor behind the sofa.

"Hi. I'm Mitch McCain." One hand held a

106

brown-leather jacket slung over his shoulder. With his other hand, he pumped Joe's arm. "Fast News Fifty-seven."

"Oh, Mr. McClain," Ellen said.

"Mc*Cain,*" he said, correcting her. "I'm looking for Ellen Talbot."

"I'm Ellen Talbot," Ellen said, casually blocking the entrance to the living room.

As he shook her hand, he peered around her and into the room. "I got your name from the employees at the *Chronicle.* They thought since you're Wanda's best friend, you might be able to tell me something about her."

"Right." Stepping aside, Ellen motioned McCain and the cameraman in. "I hope you're ready to set the record straight about Wanda."

Mr. McCain smiled slyly as he entered. "Absolutely . . ."

"Ellen! Don't believe him!" Wishbone warned, belly-crawling around the sofa to keep out of sight. When he thought it was safe, he peered out.

Behind Mr. McCain was the cameraman, carrying the large camera on his shoulder and a big blue case in his hand.

Eyeing the room, Mr. McCain nodded toward the dining room. Joe, Sam, Ellen, and the cameraman followed him as he stepped up to the table. With a brush of his hand, he pushed Ellen's paperwork aside.

"Uh . . ." Ellen's eyebrows shot up.

Wishbone jerked his head back behind the sofa. "Oh, no! Every time this guy shows up, bad stuff happens. Hey!" He spotted his squeaky book sticking out from between the sofa and the floor. "I think I'm just gonna grab my favorite toy and head for the backyard."

Before Wishbone was able to crawl halfway to the toy, the cameraman slammed the big blue case down on top of it. "Argh! Squeaky!" Wishbone quickly backed out of sight again, then peeked out of his hiding place.

Mitch McCain smiled at Ellen. "Why don't you just sit at the table and act natural? You, too, Joe." He looked unsurely at Sam and pointed to the wall. "Uh . . . you go stand over there."

Sam took a seat in the corner. While Mr. McCain put on his leather jacket, Ellen noticed Wanda's half-eaten apple in the fruit bowl and flipped it over so only the unbitten side showed.

It's summer, Wishbone thought. *And we're in the house. Why is this guy putting on his jacket?*

Sitting in a chair across from Ellen and Joe, Mitch McCain signaled to his cameraman to start rolling. "So, Ellen, have you always been on good terms with Wanda Gilmore?"

"Always." Ellen smiled. "Wanda Gilmore is a wonderful person, and Oakdale is very proud of all she's done."

"Yeah! Way to go, Ellen!" Wishbone whispered, still hiding next to the sofa. He stood and poked his head out farther. "Any minute now I should have a clear shot to the kitchen."

Mr. McCain scanned the room as if he were looking for something.

Wishbone stepped back.

"She's always there if someone's in trouble, or if you just need a friend to talk to," Ellen continued. "And she helps the kids in the neighborhood. . . ."

Mitch McCain turned away.

"Now!" Dropping down, Wishbone crawled as fast as he could toward the kitchen.

"She also cares a lot about the community," Ellen said.

Mitch McCain swung around. "What was that?"

"Uh-oh. I've been spotted." Wishbone made a lunge for freedom.

Ellen kept talking as if nothing unusual was happening. "She doesn't have a sneaky bone in her entire body."

"Look—it's Wishbone!" Mr. McCain jumped

up and motioned for the cameraman to aim the
camera down the back hall.

Wishbone kept going. "I'm a dust bunny. I'm
a dust bunny. I'm a dust bunny. Uh . . . 'bye." He
darted out his doggie door. "Freedom!" He flipped
in the air, then reconsidered his actions. "I can't
leave Joe and Ellen alone with that shark. I'll just
hide out here and listen." He pressed himself
against the house near the doggie door.

"What's the dog doing in your house?" Mr.
McCain asked.

"Well—"

The reporter cut off Ellen's response. "Look!
In the kitchen. That blue bowl on the floor says
'Wishbone' on it. Is Wishbone *your* dog?"

Ellen hesitated. "Well . . . yes . . . he is," she finally said. "Actually, he's Joe's dog."

"But it's like he belongs to the whole town," Joe said. "He really only sleeps here."

"Oh, really?" Mr. McCain said. "I see."

"No, he doesn't!" Wishbone warned. "His voice is oozing with suspicion. Joe, Ellen—watch out!"

The cameraman packed up his gear.

"I think we got what we came for. Thank you, Ellen and Joe. You can see yourselves on the evening news," Mr. McCain said, his voice getting fainter as he headed toward the front door.

"Good-bye, Mr. McCain," Ellen said.

Then Wishbone heard the front door open and shut. He listened for a minute to make sure the only footsteps in the house belonged to Joe, Ellen, and Sam. Then he pushed back inside through his doggie door. "Boy, am I glad that's over! All that hiding has made me really, really hungry, Ellen. How about a snack?" He sat up.

"I *think* the interview went well. I'll see if anyone wants to meet down at Pepper Pete's and watch the news, like we did last Sunday." Ellen picked up the phone. "Hearing all the good things about herself should cheer Wanda up."

"Good idea," Joe and Sam said at the same time.

"I know we just had pizza," Ellen said. "Do

111

you mind, Joe? We can always order salads if you're tired of pizza."

Joe smiled. "Are you kidding? I'll eat pizza any day of the week!"

"Helllooo!" Wishbone trotted over and begged in front of Joe. "Pizza sounds fine for later, but right now the cute canine would like a ginger snap."

That evening, Ellen, Joe, and Wishbone met Hank, Travis, Melina, and Marcus at Pepper Pete's. They sat at the tables nearest the TV, ordered, and watched the last few minutes of a show on travel.

"Wow! Do I love the smell of pizza!" Wishbone held his nose high and sniffed, then put it to the floor and wandered off. "The Wishbone Crumbmaster at your service," he said, coming across edible tidbits near some other customers.

As the travel show ended and the news started, Melina looked around. "Where's Miss Gilmore?"

"She couldn't make it," Ellen said. She signaled to Walter and Sam, who were behind the counter getting drinks for everyone, to join them. "Unfortunately, when I phoned her, she said she already had made other plans."

"Hey! Wait for me," Wishbone said, trotting back to join the others when he heard Helen Davidson's voice on the news. Finding a good spot, he sat down and watched her.

"And now, Mitch McCain's Fast News Fifty-seven investigative report: 'Wanda Gilmore: Local Hero—or Town Tyrant?'"

"What?" Joe said, as everyone gasped in surprise. "How can they say that about Miss Gilmore?"

Wishbone walked around the table and sat next to Joe. "Wanda has never hesitated to let me know she doesn't appreciate my digging abilities, but I'd never call her a *tyrant.*"

The TV again showed the scene of the screaming glee club members and the collapsing light grid. Then the scene cut to Wanda with Melina after the rescue.

Suddenly, the screen was filled with Mitch McCain's head and shoulders.

"Boy, he wears that same brown-leather jacket whether it's hot or cold, day or night," Wishbone said. "He may think it's something great, but his coat's not nearly as nice as mine. Why, his doesn't have even one spot on it!"

"Thank you, Helen," Mitch said, smiling before putting on a more serious look. "We watched in awe as Wanda Gilmore rescued young Melina

Finch from the wreckage of the collapsing stage at the summer carnival. But there appears to be a flip side—dark side—to Wanda Gilmore."

More murmurs and gasps went up from the tables.

"I can't believe this man!" Ellen said.

Mr. McCain spoke in a low, even voice. "We talked to some of her employees down at the *Chronicle*."

"Look," Walter said. He pointed to the screen as the news story cut to a scene inside the *Chronicle* offices. It showed the employees bustling around as they worked.

Wishbone put a paw on Joe's leg. "See that woman in the white blouse? That's the woman Mr. McCain interviewed just before he interviewed Wanda. Watch—she'll help set things straight!"

"Well, everybody works very hard here," the woman said into the mike. "Wanda always says if you don't want to work hard, you might be happier someplace else." She frowned. "Excuse me."

"That's not how it happened!" Wishbone blurted out. But all of his friends seemed too stunned to notice. He trotted from table to table trying to explain. "People! They cut out what the woman said about Wanda just before that. She said Wanda was the hardest worker of all!"

The news story cut to Mr. McCain again. "And Travis Del Rio told us about Wanda's stranglehold on the local business community."

"What!" the Travis at Pepper Pete's said, nearly spilling his soft drink.

Wishbone took a seat and watched the Travis on TV.

"She . . . uh . . . she loaned me the start-up money to open Oakdale Sports and Games. She also helped Walter Kepler start his business, Pepper Pete's. She owns the building."

"So she owns Pepper Pete's, too?" Mr. McCain sounded surprised.

"Well . . . yes—the building." Travis raised his eyebrows. "I'm sorry. I thought everyone knew that."

"And in return," Mitch McCain said, pulling part of a newspaper from his jacket pocket, "Travis is forced to advertise in *her* newspaper. He's unable to take advantage of television's ability to reach more people."

"I don't believe a word of it!" Wishbone said, jumping up to all fours and looking around at the tables. "Whoa! By the looks on your faces, you guys don't, either. This Mitch McCain is just a big rat! Now, who's got a big rat trap?"

Mitch McCain stepped closer to the camera. "And what about the dog she claimed was hers? We visited Wanda's neighbor, Ellen Talbot, in her house. Let's hear what she has to say about this."

The news story flashed to a close-up of Wishbone's blue bowl in the Talbots' kitchen. Then the scene cut to the very end of Ellen's interview with Mr. McCain: "Actually, he's Joe's dog," Ellen said.

"He really only sleeps here," Joe added.

Mitch McCain's face was the focus of the camera again. "Wanda Gilmore has even persuaded Wishbone's real owners to go along with her scheme."

Ellen, from her chair in Pepper Pete's, frowned at the TV set. "He purposely left out part of the conversation."

The picture cut back to the newsroom, to

anchorperson Helen Davidson. "Wow! That's interesting," she said. "You wouldn't think such an upstanding citizen would be so deceptive."

"I know what you mean, Helen," Mitch McCain said.

"But tell me, Mitch, what is the latest piece of information you've uncovered on Wanda Gilmore?"

The news story cut to Mitch McCain again. "Well, Helen, I'm standing here on beautiful historic Oak Street in front of the now infamous *Oakdale Chronicle*. We have been able to uncover city records that show, without a doubt, that Wanda Gilmore actually owns *every* building on this block!" He paused. "Does Wanda Gilmore have her own secret plans for downtown Oakdale?" His hand swept the air behind him. "As she tries to possess it all, will there soon be a four-story shopping mall on Oak Street? Maybe the public already thinks so. . . . Here with me is Mr. Leon King, a law-abiding local citizen in the community."

The group at Pepper Pete's groaned as the camera view widened to show a broad-shouldered Mr. King standing beside Mitch McCain. His slightly graying hair was neatly parted, and his dark blue suit was wrinkle-free and spotless.

"I've known about this woman for years,"

Mr. King said. "If something doesn't make money for Wanda Gilmore, it doesn't get done in this town!"

"Unbelievable!" Ellen put a hand to her face.

Wishbone glanced at his friends. Then he looked back at Leon King's dressed-to-impress look. Wishbone lowered his voice. "Today on *Wishbone Live:* Never trust someone just because he wears his Sunday best."

The picture cut back to the newsroom. "Tune in tomorrow," Helen Davidson said, "to learn more about the real reasons behind the secret dealings of Wanda Gilmore. Is she the local hero, or the town tyrant? This is Helen Davidson, for Fast News Fifty-seven."

"That's ridiculous!" Walter pulled the TV remote control from his pocket and punched off the set.

Ellen shook her head. "The news station has taken everything out of context!"

"And it's all been completely turned around." Joe reached down to pet Wishbone.

"I don't believe the guy just did that," Sam said. She looked at Melina. "Your hunch about him was right."

"Believe it, Sam." Wishbone scratched his ear. "I've seen this guy in action, and it's not pretty."

Marcus tapped Travis on the shoulder. "Uncle Travis, is Miss Gilmore really the town tyrant?"

"Yeah—does she really *make* you advertise in her paper?" Melina asked.

Travis seemed upset. "Oh, no, not at all. You have to understand that Mr. McCain can twist everything around."

"They make her sound so *horrible*," Sam said.

Walter put a hand on his daughter's shoulder. "Sam, Wanda's the best landlord anyone could want. You know how easy she made it for us to take over Pepper Pete's."

"Your father's right, Sam," Ellen said. "There was nothing sneaky or illegal about what Wanda did. She kept alive her father's dream of preserving the beauty and the history of Oakdale. And that's all there is to it."

"Yeah." Wishbone wagged his tail. "Why should someone get in trouble for helping out friends?"

Long Bill Longley has gone out on a limb to help his friend, Tom Merwin. And it looks as if there's a giant fall waiting for him, too.

Chapter Nine

The following day, Tom showed up at Long Bill's office at noon, as usual. "Lunchtime, Bill."

"Sorry, Tom," Long Bill said, standing in his wooden chair to stretch his legs. "I can't make it today. Something mighty important's come up." *Something mighty important—like going over your bank loan with a fine-toothed flea comb, looking for a way that could save both our necks.* "Say, you haven't heard anything from Ed yet, have you?"

Tom shook his head. "Nope—not yet. I guess he'll be along any day now." He poked a finger at the brim of his hat, pushing it up. "I'm disappointed you'll be missing out on lunch, Bill. I have a feeling that after yesterday, Mame's gonna be feelin' a mite unfriendly."

Long Bill wagged his tail. "I have a feeling you're right, partner."

With a quick nod good-bye, Tom left the bank. Long Bill pulled out Tom's loan agreement and went to work. He spent several hours reading it over and over, looking for any scrap of information that would satisfy J. Edgar Todd.

"Nothing!" he barked, sighing deeply and sitting back down in his chair. "I've looked at these words so much they've become a blur. Maybe it's time I get myself something to eat." Using his teeth, he pulled out his pocket watch. "Why, in an hour it'll be closing time. No wonder I'm so doggone hungry."

Long Bill put on his derby and trotted out to the boardwalk. As he started toward Mame's, something caught his eye. On a bench in front of the stable sat Tom Merwin, braiding a riding whip. "Hmm . . . Something must be up. Tom usually goes straight back to work after lunch."

Long Bill walked down the steps, waited for a wagon to pass, then trotted across the dirt street. He jumped up on the bench next to Tom. "How do, Tom? Did something bad happen at Mame's?"

Tom shook his head. "Naw." He looked up from his braiding. "What's gonna happen with the loan, Bill?"

Long Bill sat on his haunches, trying to get his back out of the hot sun. "Well, I checked the paperwork. Technically speaking, that bank examiner is right about your loan."

Tom frowned.

One of the horses in the stable neighed, as if he knew what Long Bill was talking about.

"Now, you and I know that the loan is on the level, Tom. But that nitpicking J. Edgar Todd looked at it and says it isn't on the up-and-up."

Tom tugged the front of his hat down to keep the sun from getting to his eyes. "So what exactly does that mean?"

"Well," Long Bill said, "if I don't have the money by noon tomorrow, I suppose it means I'm gonna get jumped on by both of Uncle Sam's feet. The government will have a field day with me."

A determined look crossed Tom's face. "Don't worry, Bill. I'll raise the money for you on time."

For some reason, Tom's words did not reassure Long Bill. In fact, the remark made the fur on the back of his neck stand straight up. *How can Tom "raise" ten thousand dollars in less than twenty-four hours?* "I know you would if you could, Tom."

Tom sighed and stared off toward an unused wagon wheel, looking thoughtful.

"I'm on my way to Mame's for some food," Long Bill said. "Care to join me?"

Tom shook his head. "Nah. I've got some thinkin' to do, Bill. I can do it better all by my lonesome."

Long Bill jumped off the bench. "Tomorrow for lunch, then."

"Tomorrow," Tom echoed.

That cowpoke's up to something, Long Bill thought as he walked away. *I can sense it.* Sure enough, when he looked back, Tom was putting away his half-finished whip.

Long Bill ducked out of sight behind a water trough and watched.

Tom put his whip in his saddlebag, then hurried up the street. He made a beeline to the office of Cooper & Craig, the land-management office in town. First he looked both ways, as if he was making sure no one could see him. Then he darted inside.

"He's acting mighty suspicious," Long Bill said to himself. At his first chance, Long Bill raced across the street, then ducked under the window of Cooper & Craig's office. Hiding in the shadow of the water barrel out front, he listened. He easily picked up the conversation inside, thanks to his sharp hearing.

Tom was explaining his loan situation to someone. When Long Bill's instincts told him it was safe, he slowly rose up on his hind legs. Resting his front paws against the siding, he peeked in the window.

Tom, his hat in his lap, sat with his back to Long Bill. To Tom's left, facing the side wall, sat Cooper, the president of the land-management office. Cooper wore a fancy jacket and sat behind an ornate, hand-carved wooden desk. On one side of him there was a shiny black safe.

Cooper frowned from behind his gold, wire-rimmed glasses. "What was Long Bill thinking? He is president of the First National Bank!" Cooper tapped the desk with his fingertips to stress his words. "There are government rules and such. He had no right putting through such an improper loan."

Things aren't always done by the book, Coop, Long Bill thought. *Especially when the darned book has more rules than a stray cat has fleas.*

"So, you gonna help me out, Coop?" Tom's voice was hopeful.

The president stiffened and took on a professional manner, one that lacked any sign of friendship.

Long Bill's tail drooped.

Tom held up one hand, as if he expected his palm to stop any words he didn't want to hear. "Now, don't say no. I owe that money on a call loan. It's been called, and the man who called it is a man I've shared the same blanket with in cow camps for ten years." Tom began to tap his boot on the floor. "He's got to have the money—and I've got to get it for him."

Cooper looked down at his desk, avoiding Tom's eyes. He shook his head. "Well, I wish I could, Tom, but I have a partner, you know. Besides that, we're making a shipment of fifteen thousand dollars to Myer Brothers in Rockdell to buy cotton with." He finally looked up. "It goes out on the first stagecoach tomorrow, at dawn. So, you see, that leaves our cash on hand quite short."

Tom sighed. "I see."

"Sorry we can't arrange anything for you," Cooper said.

Pushing himself to his feet, Tom gave a quick nod. Then he turned toward the door.

Long Bill dropped down just in time to keep from being seen. His heart skipped a beat. *That was a close one*, he thought, squeezing behind the water barrel to keep from being discovered by Tom.

Long Bill stuck his nose in the crack between the building and the barrel and looked out.

A second later Tom stepped out of the office, looking discouraged. He glanced up and down the boardwalk, then up again. He snapped his fingers and was on the verge of a smile. Suddenly he took off up the walk, his boots banging against the boards as he went.

When Tom had a good head start, Long Bill sneaked after him, ducking into the alley near the general store. He peered out. Tom had come to a stop in front of the store.

George was crouched down out front, unloading china dishes and kerosene lamps from a wagon.

"Howdy, George," Tom said, looking at his back.

Long Bill wagged his tail. *Once again I'm within hearing distance. Lucky dog!*

George glanced up over his shoulder. "Howdy, Tom."

Tom stuck his thumbs in his belt loops. "Ya know, George, I got this cattle deal goin'. It's gonna come through any day now."

"Is that so?" George put the glass tops on the kerosene lamps and started lining them up against the storefront for display.

"Yup." He nodded. "But, ya see, I need some advance money to cover a loan I took out from Long Bill."

"Oh?" George kept right on working, his back to Tom.

"If you could lend me the money up front— ten thousand bucks—I can almost double that return for ya in a few days."

George suddenly looked up at Tom, wide-eyed as a watchdog on duty. "Ten thousand . . . dollars?"

Tom nodded excitedly.

Catching the excitement, Long Bill wagged his tail. *That'll keep me out of Uncle Sam's doghouse.*

"I don't have that kind of money," George said.

Long Bill's ears and tail drooped, but he wasn't surprised by George's response.

Frustrated, Tom kicked at the boardwalk and sighed.

George turned his attention back to his

dishes. He stacked the glassware next to the lamps. "Is Long Bill in some sort of trouble, Tom?"

Tom's forehead wrinkled in a frown. "Oh, it's that dang bank examiner who's come to town and called in my loan. If I don't pay that money back pronto, it's gonna be on Bill's head for givin' it to me in the first place."

"Well, I'm sure sorry to hear Long Bill's in trouble with the government. . . ." George's voice drifted off.

Not half as sorry as I am, Long Bill thought. *And Tom looks desperate. I suppose I should get him off the hook—tell him not to worry about the loan. But if he can find a way to set things right before J. Edgar Todd returns, it sure would be a load off my furred hide. I don't cotton to the idea of spending time in a flea-infested jail.*

Suddenly Tom spun around, forcing Long Bill to jerk his head back. By the sound of the footsteps, Tom was coming back his way! Long Bill glanced down the alley he was in. There was nothing to hide behind. The footsteps were getting closer.

In one swift move, Long Bill flattened himself against the side of the building. His heart pounded—it seemed *so* loud, but he knew Tom's ears would never hear it. He kept very quiet until

Tom passed by and he was sure he'd gone unnoticed.

Long Bill relaxed. He let his tongue hang out and, for a few seconds, took quick, noisy breaths. Then, peeking around the corner, he was surprised to see Tom stop in front of Cooper & Craig's office again.

Tom stared in the office window. Finally, shoulders sagging, head shaking, he walked away.

That's a powerful look of desperation, Long Bill thought. *I'm afraid Tom has reached the end of his rope. Darn that J. Edgar Todd!*

Long Bill proceeded to follow Tom up the street. He padded softly on all four feet, ducking out of sight whenever the need arose. From behind a flowerpot containing dry dirt and the remains of a dead plant, Long Bill watched as Tom walked to his horse. Grabbing the saddle horn and putting his left boot in the stirrup, Tom mounted up.

Something's not right, Long Bill thought. *I can feel it in my bones*. When Tom left, Long Bill hightailed it back toward Cooper & Craig. "'Scuse me. Coming through," he said to the folks on the boardwalk. There sure seemed to be a lot of people out. "'Scuse me. Man on a mission." Long Bill finally reached Cooper &

Craig. He looked in the window. Cooper was unloading money out of the safe and putting it into a chest.

Hmm . . . Long Bill made a run for his horse. He jumped up on the water barrel in front and then onto Ginger.

"Uh . . . excuse me," he said to Daniel Lawson, who was passing by, "I seem to have forgotten to get my reins. Could you hand them to me?"

Daniel nodded politely. Without a word, he unwound the leather straps from the hitching post and handed them to Long Bill.

"Thank you, thir," he said when the leather straps were securely in his mouth. Then he turned Ginger and galloped out of town to follow Tom. There wasn't much to hide him on the road, so he lagged behind, then used his nose to follow Tom's scent. He was surprised to find out that Tom had headed straight home.

"Maybe I was plumb wrong," Long Bill said as he reached Tom's ranch.

He took cover behind Tom's weathered barn after Tom had bedded his horse down and gone into the house.

"Hmm . . ." Long Bill looked around, hoping to spot a barrel or a woodpile near the barn to help him dismount from Ginger. "Nothing. Oh, well . . ."

He turned on his stomach and slid back-feet-first down the side of the saddle. When the leather ended, he dropped to the ground.

"Ouch! That smarts." Long Bill danced around on his stinging paws.

Finally, he sat down and stared at Tom's place. Dusk was approaching. Inside, Tom lit a lamp. Despite the warm summer evening, Long Bill shivered.

"All is not well with Tom Merwin. My instincts tell me to curl up here for the night and sleep with one eye open."

So, finding a tree stump, he led Ginger over to it. Jumping up on it, Long Bill stood on his hind legs and nosed through his saddlebag. He grabbed items in his teeth. First he pulled out his chaps, then a comfortable shirt, his leather vest, and then his cowboy hat.

"I may as well get comfy," he said, removing his banker's clothes.

That night, Long Bill hid behind Tom Merwin's barn. He slept a few hours and rose early, waiting for Tom to make some sort of move. It came at daybreak.

Tom walked outside, placing his cowboy hat on his head. He quickly saddled up his horse and took off like a bullet.

"Let's go, Ginger!" Long Bill said as he mounted his horse. "Giddap!"

He raced along the trail toward Tom's dust cloud.

"Why is he in such a cotton-pickin' hurry?" Long Bill wondered aloud. "He's acting like he's late for his own wedding."

All of a sudden, Tom turned off the trail and raced across the thicket, dodging balls of sagebrush. For some reason he was riding straight toward the stagecoach route.

Slowing a bit, Long Bill began to add things up: *the look of desperation Tom had when he looked in the window and saw Cooper unloading money from the safe . . . the fact that Tom needed money . . . and now this shortcut to the stagecoach route.*

Long Bill checked his pocket watch and became alarmed. "Oh, no! This is going to be a really close call."

With a kick of his hind paws and a click of his tongue, he urged Ginger into a run. "Come on, girl! Tom is headed for big trouble."

He leaned forward and hung on to the saddle horn as Ginger's hooves beat the ground beneath him. The smell of sage and dust filled his black nostrils.

Reining to the right, Long Bill led Ginger off Tom's trail. "We need our own shortcut if we're going to make it in time."

As Long Bill raced toward the stagecoach route, he saw Tom up the trail. Tom was off his horse, crouching behind a bush. The sun was all the way up now, full daylight. Long Bill tried to hide behind mesquite trees to keep from being seen, but they were few and far between.

He suddenly heard the rattle of the stagecoach wheels, then saw six horses running full speed, pulling it over the rise. Next, Long Bill saw Tom tie a neckerchief over his nose and mouth.

"Oh, no!"

Long Bill raced forward, Ginger's hooves pounding the ground.

"Go, go, go!" he barked.

Tom and Long Bill are sure in a tight spot! Speaking of being caught in a tight spot, let's go back to Oakdale and see how Wanda's doing. . . .

Chapter Ten

With his head resting comfortably on Joe's lap, Wishbone was enjoying an evening rest on the sofa in the Talbots' living room. Then he fell asleep and began to dream. Something or someone was trying to make a snack of his ears. He heard neighing. "No, horsey! Bad horse!" He pawed the air, trying to keep the horse from nibbling his ears. Suddenly Wishbone awoke, bolted to a sitting position, and looked around.

"What's the matter, boy?" Joe asked, giving him a reassuring pat. "Don't you like your ears scratched while you're sleeping?"

Wishbone cocked his head. The horse sounds were still coming . . . he looked around . . . his eyes focused on the TV. "Oh—it's a western," he said, relieved.

Behind him, he heard Ellen and Wanda in the

study. As he circled the sofa cushion to get comfortable again, he saw them. Wanda, with her shoes off, lounged on the sofa in there, while Ellen sat nearby in her desk chair.

Ellen was telling Wanda all about how Mitch McCain was acting when he came to the house to interview her that morning.

"Unbelievable!" Wanda wriggled her toes.

Ellen nodded. "He was rude and seemed disappointed that I didn't have negative things to say about you."

"What did he say? What did he say?" Wanda reached up and fingered a blouse button near her neck.

Ellen put her hands on her lap. "Well, first of all, he took all of my stuff off the table and just . . ."

Wishbone's head snapped around as Joe clicked the remote to change channels and caught the beginning of a news story. A slow-motion clip of Wanda saving Melina came onscreen, then a photograph of Wanda, then a shot of a copy of *The Oakdale Chronicle*. Finally, there was a shot of money passing hands, implying a shady deal, and Wanda's picture filled the screen and stayed there.

An unseen announcer spoke: "We all watched as Wanda Gilmore performed her heroic deed that day. But who were we *really* watching? Did we know we were watching Wanda Gilmore, secret landlord of downtown Oakdale? No."

Wanda and Ellen heard the news story, and hurried out of the study to join Joe and Wishbone in the living room.

Wanda stared at the television screen, wide-eyed as the announcer continued.

"Does Wanda Gilmore rightfully own *The Oakdale Chronicle* or the building it resides in? Did her father, Giles Gilmore, gain ownership of *The Oakdale Chronicle* by swindling its previous owner? Could property-snatching be a family tradition? Tune in tonight for the *full* story."

Wishbone watched Ellen and Wanda exchange stunned looks.

"Now they're going after my father! And he's dead!" Wanda said. "What did I ever do to them?"

Ellen sounded sympathetic. "Wanda, do you know how your father got the paper?"

"I don't know." Wanda looked baffled. "I wasn't even born then."

Wishbone bowed his head. "Next the TV station will be saying *my* papers are forged."

The next morning Joe grabbed two apples from the fruit bowl as he passed through the dining room. "Hey! What's this?" A business card was by the fruit bowl. Holding both apples in one hand, Joe picked up the card. He groaned as he read it. "Mitch McCain, Fast News Fifty-seven, Investigative Reporter." With a sigh, Joe slipped the card into his T-shirt pocket. "Yeah, right."

"I sense you don't really mean that," Wishbone said, following him toward the front hall. "'Yeah, right,' means 'yeah, right, I don't believe a word of it.'"

Wishbone was the first one out when Joe pulled open the door.

"Sunshine! What a fine Wednesday morning." He raced in a circle around the yard, then stopped. "And Sam!" He wagged his tail at top speed as he watched her riding up on her bike.

"Hi, Wishbone." She got off, then straightened the straps of her short denim overalls. As she bent to give Wishbone a quick scratch, her blond ponytail flopped forward. She pushed it back and then went over and sat down next to Joe on the porch steps.

She smiled when he handed her an apple. Joe gave her a weak smile in return.

"What's the matter, Joe?" Sam bit into her apple.

138

"Mailman's here!" Wishbone barked out, as the mail carrier, Dan Bloodgood, approached.

"I couldn't help hearing the news on TV," Dan said, sorting through the mail in his hand, then passing a stack to Joe. "You okay, Joe?"

Joe pulled Mitch McCain's business card from his pocket and held it up for Sam and Dan to read. Then he told them about the news story from the night before. "I don't understand why the TV station is doing this to Miss Gilmore."

Dan rested a foot on the bottom step. "Well, Joe, there are journalists who think some things are more newsworthy than others—even if the story might end up hurting someone."

Wishbone sniffed the mailman's shoe. "Hey! You've been to Sparky's already. Did he give you any messages for me?"

Sam took the business card from Joe and read it again. "I wish we could do something to help Miss Gilmore."

"What could *we* do?" Joe asked. "Fast News Fifty-seven is a big TV station."

"You'd be surprised what just a few people can do—especially when they know the truth," Dan Bloodgood said, walking away.

Sam looked at Joe. "But what if Miss Gilmore really doesn't own the *Chronicle?*"

Joe pushed himself up off the steps. "Maybe we need to do a little investigating of our own."

"I love investigating. My nose was made for it!" Wishbone wagged his tail. "Where do we start?"

Sam stood. "Where do we start?"

"Hey! I asked first," Wishbone said.

"Well." Joe raised his brows. "Mom always says if you're not sure where to start, start at the library."

"Get your bike, and let's go see your mom at the library," Sam said, getting on her bike.

"Oh, good!" Wishbone stood next to Sam's bike and waited for Joe. "I love the library. It has such great books! It's too bad dogs aren't allowed inside—I'd be one of its best customers."

Wishbone trotted along the sidewalk as Joe and Sam pedaled their bikes. By the time they reached the library, Wishbone was out of breath. "It's so hot, Joe. Let me go inside. Please? I'll be good. I promise."

Joe locked his bike in the rack, then looked around the grounds of the Henderson Memorial Library. Joe wiped his forehead with his arm. "It's so hot here, and there isn't any shade. I have to take Wishbone inside. I hope Mom doesn't get upset."

Sam smiled. "I think she'll understand."

Once inside, they searched out Ellen.

"Oh, Joe." Ellen looked at Wishbone. "You know Wishbone is not supposed to be in here."

"But I forgot his leash. And there isn't any shade out there for him."

Ellen sighed and gave Wishbone a *mom* look. "You better behave yourself or . . . or . . . or no ginger snaps for a month!"

"A whole month!" Wishbone couldn't believe his ears. "Don't you think that's a little harsh?" He looked around at all the interesting places he could investigate.

Ellen continued to stare down at him.

"Oh, all right. I promise." Wishbone sat perfectly still and waited for Sam and Joe as they explained their situation to Ellen.

She led them into the microfiche room and gestured with her hand. "Back along this wall are the books on Oakdale."

"I'll start with the books," Joe said.

"Okay. I'll investigate the microfiche files." Sam followed Ellen to the files.

Ellen ran her finger down the paper holder and stopped about a third of the way down. "I think what you're looking for starts about here, Sam."

"Thanks, Mrs. Talbot." As Sam started to read the headings, Ellen left.

"Aha!" Wishbone found a microfiche viewer

with two chairs in front of it and jumped into one. He watched Joe carry a stack of books to the table behind him, then sit down. "You know, Joe, being good is very, very boring. Joe?" Wishbone sighed. Joe was busy turning pages in one of the books.

"My best friend won't even listen to me." Wishbone turned back around and looked for a way to occupy himself, yet stay out of trouble. He sniffed the machine. "Oh, look. Someone left some film in here."

He put his paw on the viewer lever and pushed it. The information raced past his eyes in a blur.

"Paper goes up." Wishbone pushed the lever the other way. "Paper goes down." He moved the

lever again. "Paper goes up." He continued playing. "Paper goes down . . . paper goes up. . . . Ha-ha! I could do this all day! Paper goes down. . . ."

He heard Sam's footsteps coming his way.

"Okay, Wishbone, stop playing around," she said. She gently nudged him to the other chair, then removed the film spool that was in the machine.

"Oh, you guys get to have all the fun," Wishbone said, as Sam sat down in the chair directly in front of the viewer.

As Sam slid her film into the viewer, Wishbone pointed to the lever with his nose.

"Sam . . . Sam, move that little lever and watch what happens. Paper goes up! Paper goes down. Paper goes—Helllooo! Sam, you're not paying attention."

From behind Wishbone, Joe sighed. "Find anything yet?"

"Not really." Sam continued looking at the film—it was front pages from *The Oakdale Chronicle*.

Joe grunted. "There's no mention of the sale of the newspaper in this history book, either. We're really coming up empty, you know."

"Wait a minute." Sam moved back and forth between two front pages and pointed to the owner's name on each front page. "On May 21,

1932, the owner was Abel Skelton." She moved to the next day's paper. "On May 22, 1932, the paper is listed as being owned and operated by Giles Gilmore."

Wishbone heard footsteps. "Oh, it's Ellen!" He sat perfectly still. "I'm being good. I'm being good. I'm being good . . ."

Ellen brought over a piece of film and handed it to Sam. "I found the Twenty-fifth Anniversary Special Edition of *The Oakdale Chronicle*. Maybe there's something useful in it."

As Sam slipped one piece of film out of the viewer and put the other one in, Joe came and stood behind her chair.

Ellen smiled and waved to someone in the doorway. "Here comes Melina."

"Hi, Mrs. Talbot." She carried two paperbacks in her hand. "Oh, hi, Joe. Hi, Sam. What are you guys doing here? And Wishbone!" She sounded surprised.

"Don't worry, I'm being good," Wishbone said.

Joe nodded at the viewer. "We're trying to find a way to help Miss Gilmore."

He and Ellen leaned down for a better view. Melina joined them at Sam's left shoulder.

"Ooh, come on!" Wishbone couldn't contain himself any longer; he wriggled. "It's my turn! Paper goes up! Paper goes down!"

Sam continued to maneuver the lever until she located the front page of the paper. "Here it is," she said.

"Oh, look, there's a picture of some men dressed in funny clothes," Wishbone said. "Plus a lady in funny clothes."

Ellen squinted. "The caption says '1951.'"

"Look." Sam pointed to one of the men in the picture. "The caption identifies this man as Miss Gilmore's father."

Joe put his hands on the back of Sam's chair. "But who are all those other people?"

Ellen pressed her lips together as she thought. "I'm not sure, but I know that's Ethan Johnstone." She pointed.

"That's Hank's grandfather," Sam said. "Hey, maybe Hank can help us out." She looked at Ellen. "Is there a way to get a print out of this?"

"Sure." Ellen removed the sheet of film from the machine. "I'll be right back."

Sam turned the viewer light off. "Would you like to come with us, Melina? We can use all the help we can get."

"I'll say," Joe added.

Melina smiled. "Sure, I'll help."

"You wouldn't need any help if you let me do more," Wishbone said, glancing at the lever on the microfiche machine. "Trust me."

Wanda took a deep breath and tried to act normal as she entered the *Chronicle* building. She was hoping to slip up to her office unnoticed by her staff. But right away Caroline jumped up from her desk and stopped her. The other employees gathered around her, too.

"Wanda!" Caroline rested a hand on her shoulder. "I'm so glad you're here. Tell us, what's going on?"

"We've been getting calls all day!" Dorrie said.

Caroline nodded and raised her brows. "What's this about you not owning *The Oakdale Chronicle?*"

"How are we supposed to respond to these accusations?" Dorrie asked. "What do you want us to say?"

Wanda's head was spinning with all the questions being thrown at her. "Please, everyone, there's nothing to worry about. Let's get back to work." She continued past the desks, toward the stairs. Ginny, a crackerjack reporter, stepped in front of her boss. Wanda stopped. She could tell by Ginny's face that she wasn't going to let this matter drop.

"Wanda, this is a story," Ginny said. "We're going to have to run something in the paper about it. I need to ask you—Do you own *The Oakdale Chronicle,* or don't you?"

Suddenly Wanda felt drained, as if she hadn't slept for a week. "Well, of course I own the paper, Ginny." She was tired. "Please. I just need some time to think all this through."

Hank stepped forward from the back of the room and approached her carefully. "Miss Gilmore, is there any way that I can help?"

This time Wanda managed to show a small smile. "Thanks, Hank. Now, I'm sure this will all get straightened out and we can go back to the way things used to be."

"I'm afraid that can't happen, Wanda," said a soft voice behind her as the front door clicked shut.

Wanda turned to see Leon King inside the doorway. Neatly dressed in a gray suit, white shirt, and red tie, he stood with a hand behind his back.

Wanda let out a deep sigh and set her purse on a nearby desk. "Leon King. What do you want?"

Leon brought his hand from behind his back. It held a plant in full bloom. "For you."

A smile brightened Wanda's face as she took the plant. "A pink cyclamen! Well, how beautiful!" Then her good sense took over and she frowned. She knew Leon King well enough to know he was too sneaky to be nice for no reason. "What's the catch?"

"Well, I know how much you love plants, so I thought this would be a fitting going-away gift."

What's he talking about? Wanda wondered. "Who's going away?"

"You are." Mr. King pulled a piece of paper from the inside pocket of his suit jacket and handed it to Wanda.

Puzzled, she glanced at her employees, unfolded the paper, and began to read.

"That's a copy of a purchase-and-sale agreement," he said. "You see, *I* am now the rightful owner of *The Oakdale Chronicle.*"

Wanda felt the blood drain from her face. She stared at Leon in disbelief. "What are you talking about?"

"I did a little checking, Wanda. According to town records, the *Chronicle* building is still listed in the name of Abel Skelton. All I had to do was find Skelton's living relative and buy it from him." Mr. King smiled. "*Legally* buy it, I might add."

Wanda felt her anger rise. "Now, you see here, my father built this paper—"

"Your father . . . Please! Your father never owned *The Oakdale Chronicle*," Leon King said. "There is no telling what kind of shady deal he made with Skelton." King looked around the room. "The beauty of this situation is that I wouldn't have even known about the rightful ownership if you hadn't become Oakdale's newest hero."

Wanda's shoulders sagged as she stared at the agreement. The words blurred together. "That Mitch McCain is really something."

"He should be." Mr. King smiled again. "I pay him enough."

"What!" Wanda looked up in surprise. "You *own* that TV station?"

A sly grin crossed Mr. King's face. "As well as two others. So, don't worry, Wanda, *your* paper is in the hands of an experienced newsman."

Her heart beating fast, Wanda locked eyes with Leon King. "I own this newspaper. Plus, I won't turn this paper over to your kind of 'journalism'! You don't deal in facts—you deal in lies just to get more people to watch your newscasts so you can make more money." She pushed the plant back at him. "There must be *something* I can do!"

"Oh, there is, Wanda," Mr. King said, smiling. Then he gritted his teeth and hissed, "Get out of my newspaper! You've got until the end of the day." He turned and walked to the front door, then looked back at the employees. "I'll be back then to decide who else goes," he said. Then he swiftly walked out the door.

For a moment after the door closed, everyone stood frozen to the floor, stunned by Leon King's visit.

Wanda silently counted to ten to calm herself. "You're right, Ginny." Wanda motioned with her hand, pointing out all the equipment in the room. "We're in the news business, and *this* is news. Run a story for tomorrow, Thursday. . . . Excuse me," she said quietly. She picked up her purse and made her way through the group.

Wanda walked numbly up to her office and just stood there silently for a while, looking out the windows. Her heart sank as she glanced at the agreement. Leon King had proof—proof her father had never owned the paper. . . . But that couldn't be true! She knew in her heart it wasn't. All these years she assumed the Gilmores owned the paper. What happened? How could she fight a purchase-and-sale agreement? Was it legal? Her situation seemed hopeless. . . .

With a deep sigh, Wanda went to her desk, pulled out a file, and set to work. But she couldn't concentrate. She read the first line in the file over and over, trying to get it to sink in. Then, as she stopped working and stood up to stare out over her employees, her mind wandered. What would she do without the paper?

Forty-five minutes later, Wanda still felt stunned. She got up from her desk, picked up her purse, and quietly walked down the stairs and toward the door. This time no one stopped her.

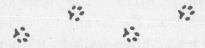

As Ellen pulled into her driveway late Wednesday afternoon, she looked over at Wanda's house. She was sitting on her porch steps surrounded by potted plants. *Something's wrong,* Ellen thought, shifting her Ford Explorer into Park. *Wanda is slouched over, her hair is a mess, and she hasn't even looked up yet. Oh, this is so unlike*

Wanda. Wanda was also unpotting flowers and flinging them aside. Something was seriously wrong.

Ellen climbed out of the sport utility vehicle and closed the door. "Wanda?" she called out.

When Wanda didn't answer, Ellen walked toward her. "Are you okay?"

"No," Wanda whispered, yanking a plant out of the pot closest to her and throwing it on the ground. She tossed the pot aside and reached for another.

As Ellen sat down on the porch steps next to her neighbor, she noticed a jar of peanut butter and a spoon in Wanda's lap. "Is there anything I can do for you?"

Staring across the yard, Wanda slowly shook her head. She tossed another plant out of a pot. "I doubt it, Ellen." Her voice was flat. "It's all a bit too late for anything, isn't it?" She pulled a spoonful of peanut butter from the jar and took a bite.

"No, it isn't." Ellen smiled. "It's never too late for your best friend."

Wanda's voice trembled. "Thanks."

Ellen put a hand on Wanda's shoulder. "Everything will work out, because you're bigger than the newspaper, Wanda. And Wanda Gilmore is so much more than what Mitch McCain tells viewers on TV. We know the *real* Wanda."

"I'm not so sure anymore, Ellen. I'm not so sure. . . ." She dropped the spoon back into the jar. Then she emptied another pot of dirt onto the ground.

What will Wanda do without *The Oakdale Chronicle?* What will become of the newspaper when it's under Leon King's control? And what does it all mean for the town of Oakdale?

Meanwhile, near Chaparosa, the situation is looking pretty bad for Tom Merwin, too. . . .

Chapter Eleven

As the stagecoach rumbled closer, Tom tipped his hat down so that it almost covered his eyes. He jumped from the thicket, pulled his gun from his holster, and fired into the air.

Spooked by the shot, the horses pulling the stagecoach raced out of control. They ran straight at Tom. Tom raised his gun again. The horses kept thundering toward him.

Long Bill grabbed his lasso. Before Tom could fire off another shot, Long Bill tossed the lasso over Tom and pulled.

"*Oof!*" Tom fell to the ground with a *thump*, his arms tied to his sides. The team of racing horses was just feet away.

Long Bill wrapped the rope once around his saddle horn and then kicked Ginger with his hind paws. "Haw!" Ginger took off, dragging Tom out

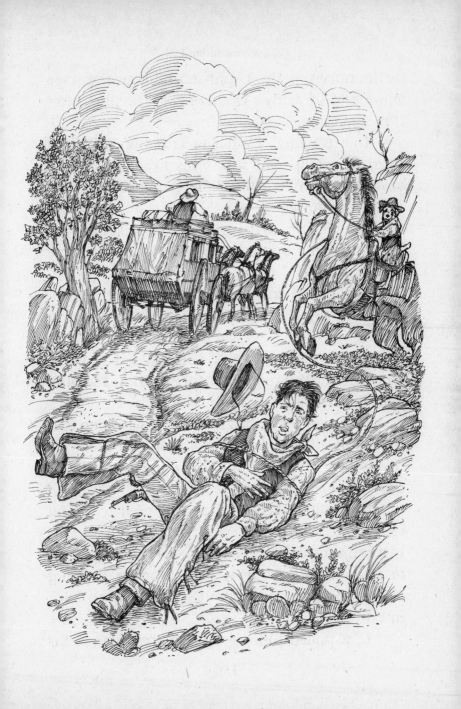

of the horses' path. A split-second later the stage thundered by. Only a cloud of dust remained after it passed safely.

Tom coughed. "What in tarnation?" Rolling over, he sat up and shook his head. He looked around, surprised. "Bill?" He loosened the rope and freed himself.

Long Bill slid to the ground and walked toward Tom. "Robbing the stagecoach isn't going to solve your problem."

Tom pulled down his neckerchief and sighed. "I'm desperate, Bill. You called your loan—I had to answer you."

His tail wagging slowly, Long Bill put a paw on Tom's arm. "You're a good friend, Tom. I admire your loyalty."

Tom glanced at the ground. "When Coop told me about all that money goin' out on the stage this morning . . . well, I didn't know what else to do."

Long Bill licked his lips and tried to sound cheerful. "Somethin'll work out," he said, his voice coming out flat. *I hope I sound more convincing to Tom than I do to myself,* he thought, trotting toward Ginger. "How about if we head on back into town?"

Tom pulled himself up and straightened his

hat. He dusted off his chaps. He gave Long Bill a hand up to his saddle, and mounted his own horse.

Long Bill clicked his tongue and turned Ginger around. He trotted toward Chaparosa, with Tom by his side.

By the time the pair reached the edge of town, the sun was a little higher.

As they approached Main Street, Tom and Long Bill slowed their horses to a walk.

Pushing his hat up off his forehead, Tom looked over at Long Bill. "What time did ya say that bank examiner was comin' back?"

"'Round noon," Long Bill said flatly. He looked up both sides of the street, noticing not too many people were out yet this morning. He shivered as he watched someone disappear into the bathhouse. Long Bill and Tom dismounted and left their horses in front of the boarding-house. *Poor fellow*, Long Bill thought. *All that soap and water, and scrub brushes, too—if it were up to me, baths would be outlawed! Why, I bet they even do nail-clipping in there.* They walked away from the boardinghouse. He turned his muzzle back toward Tom. "What about Ed? Ya think he's on his way back with the money yet?"

"He's gotta be." Tom sounded hopeful. "There ain't no two ways about it."

I wish I could be sure, Long Bill thought. *Then I'd feel a whole lot better.* "I wish we could take us a ride to find your brother. But there isn't enough time."

Tom smiled. "It would be just like old times again with the two of us out on the trail."

Long Bill felt his tail begin to wag as he thought about the old days. "We had us some darned-tootin' times, didn't we, Tom?"

Tom's eyes brightened. "We sure did, Bill. We sure did."

All of a sudden, a wild yell shattered the morning silence. "*Yeee-hawww!*"

The fur on Long Bill's neck stood on end. Long Bill's sharp gaze shot up the street. Out in front of the bank, a man, with his back to him and Tom, swayed drunkenly.

Long Bill sniffed the air and immediately recognized the scent. "Dadgummit! Calliope's at it again." People who went out and about skittered out of Calliope's way.

When Tom and Long Bill walked into the middle of the street, Calliope spun around and grinned wickedly. His teeth were as yellow as an autumn leaf. His clothes were dusty, and he hadn't bothered to shave again. The whisker stubbles all over his face made him look like a scraggly cat.

Cartridge belts with holsters attached crisscrossed his chest and circled his waist. Guns—four all together—filled the holsters, and two more pistols were tucked between his belt and his pants. Calliope pulled the Colt .45 revolvers from his belt and pointed them at a row of colored bottles that lined the fence rail near the stable.

He's got six guns! Long Bill glanced from Calliope to his own shadow, lying in the street. The morning sun coming from behind Long Bill stretched his shadow so he looked even taller than he actually was. It gave him courage.

"Oh, bury me not . . ." Calliope sang out, then paused to fire his guns. Two bottles on the rail exploded. He continued his song: ". . . on the lone prairie . . . where the coyotes howl . . . and the wind blows free . . ."

The blacksmith stepped out of the stable to see what all the noise was about.

Calliope rocked back and forth and fired two more bullets—one hit a bottle; the other struck the hammer in the blacksmith's hand. The blacksmith ducked back inside like a tortoise pulling back its head.

Long Bill ran a paw over his eye.

"I have a feeling Calliope's gonna get himself in a pack of trouble with all that ammunition."

Tom gave a quick nod. "I'm afraid you're right, Bill."

Calliope started to sing again. "In a narrow grave . . . hmm-hmm-hmm-hmm-hmm . . ." He hummed a line, then shot another bottle. "Oh, bury me not on the lone prairie . . ." Spotting Long Bill and Tom as they headed toward him, Calliope stopped singing and shoved his guns back in his belt. "Well, if it ain't the two most law-abidin' citizens of Chaparosa." He removed his hat. Attempting to bow, he nearly tumbled head over heels, and his hat flew off.

Tom held up a hand. "Why don't you just do this town a favor and crawl under a rock till you sleep this thing off?"

Teetering, Calliope plopped his hat back on his head. "I don't hafta take no orders from you, Tom Merwin. You two . . . you two strut around here like you own this dang town."

"Now, hold on just a minute." Long Bill raised a front paw in the air. "What's all this fuss about, Calliope?" He was acting as if he were the runt of the litter and getting all the abuse.

"It's just pure dang luck that you two are where you're at and I'm where I'm at." He pointed to the ground at his feet. "With a different roll o' the dice, why, I'd be wearin' yer boots right now."

Perhaps he hasn't gotten a good look at my feet lately, Long Bill thought, glancing down at his paws.

"Well, if you only worked for once in your life and saved the money instead of blowing it on cards and liquor, you *would* be wearin' boots like mine." Tom's patience seemed to be slipping away. He let out a sigh. "You see, that's what I just don't understand. How can a feller be so dang stupid—"

Calliope waved his arms wildly, making him wobble like a three-legged cat. "I'm in a fightin' mood, Tom. And I got a bullet right here . . ." He ran his hands over his cartridge belts, squinting as he tried to focus his eyes. He frowned. "I got a bullet right here . . ." He removed a bullet from his belt and almost dropped it. "Oops! It's right here, and with your name on it." He spread his feet and held his hands out to his sides above the holsters on his hips. "Tom Merwin—I'm callin' you out."

Long Bill barked. "He *is* out, Calliope."

"Well, okay." Calliope seemed satisfied by Long Bill's remark.

"All right, Calliope," Tom said, "if you want a gun fight, I'll take you up on that." He turned his head away from Calliope and winked at Long Bill. "Uh . . . why don't you count out the paces, Bill?"

"Sure thing, Tom." Long Bill ran off the street

to the boardwalk. He sat down on his haunches to watch. *I wonder what kind of trick Tom has up his sleeve for Calliope.*

Tom and Calliope eyed each other from a distance. Finally, both men started toward each other, Tom walking, and Calliope staggering.

When the two met, Long Bill rose to all fours. "All right, boys. Back to back."

As the men turned around, Calliope released a loud burp and swayed. Nearly falling over backward, he leaned on to Tom's back for support, bending Tom forward.

Frowning and grunting, Tom heaved his shoulders back, pushing Calliope upright.

Long Bill waited for Calliope to catch his balance. "Here we go. One . . . two . . . three . . ."

As Calliope swaggered away, Tom took his paces, too. A small smile curled the very corners of his lips. Instead of walking down the middle of the street, as he was supposed to, Tom changed directions and sneaked off the street toward Long Bill. Nodding for Long Bill to follow, he headed toward the partially opened door of the stable.

Long Bill trotted noiselessly, still counting so Calliope wouldn't get suspicious. "Four . . . five . . . six . . . seven . . . eight . . . nine . . ." Finally, they were at the door. *"Ten!"* Long Bill shouted, as he and Tom ran to hide inside the stable.

Long Bill crossed the cool dirt floor. Leaping up to a barrel, he put his nose into a gap between two boards in the siding and then peered out at Calliope.

Tom leaned on a nearby stack of hay bales. He watched Calliope through a knothole. "Let's see what he does."

"Maybe he'll tucker himself out." *A good old roll in the grass might calm Calliope down a bit,* Long Bill thought. *Then, again, it might make him all the more frisky.*

Calliope was spinning left and right, his guns drawn. He turned again, looking to shoot anything that moved. But the street was empty. "What's goin' on?" Calliope called. "Oh, oh, I see. Well, that's the last time you make a fool outta me . . . !" He leaned back and let out a yell. "Wooooo-hooo!" Then he started shooting again.

Calliope shot at the windmill, hit one of the blades, and started it spinning. Then he turned and unleashed five shots at the sign on the bank.

"Doggone it!" Long Bill growled. "He shot a circle all the way around the sign."

Spinning in the opposite direction, Calliope began shooting wildly.

Long Bill caught movement out of the corner of his eye. "Seems someone's comin' out of the saloon. He looks mighty confused. I hope he has enough sense to . . . duck . . . Oops! Too late," he said, as Calliope shot a liquor bottle right out of the man's hand.

As Tom shook his head, the man turned and stumbled back through the swinging doors, into the relative safety of the saloon.

"Woooo-hooo!" Calliope spun again.

A rabbi, with his hands in the air, moved carefully across the street toward Calliope, as if he wanted to try to talk to him. "I'm guessing he don't know what Calliope's really like," Tom said.

"Put the guns down," the rabbi called, continuing to advance slowly toward Calliope. "There's no need for violence." He took another small step. "Please, put the guns down."

Calliope raised his arm and took aim at the rabbi, sending the religious leader scrambling in the opposite direction.

"I'm guessing he's figured out by now what Calliope's really like." Long Bill stood on his hind legs to peer out an even bigger gap in the boards.

Mame stepped out through the swinging doors of her restaurant. Her arms were opened wide, as if she were welcoming Calliope home after a stay at the pound. In one hand she held a frying pan. "Now, Calliope, I want you to stop this foolishness immediately. Come inside." Her voice was gentle; she smiled. "I'll cook you up a nice big breakfast."

Calliope holstered his empty guns. Just as Long Bill was about to wag his tail with relief, Calliope pulled out yet another gun. Still staggering, he squeezed the trigger, hitting Mame's frying pan dead center, knocking it out of her hand.

Mame's eyes opened wide and her smile disappeared. "Well, okay." She started backing into the restaurant. "I guess that means you'll be having breakfast somewhere else today."

I can't believe Calliope did that! Long Bill thought.

Releasing another whoop, Calliope spun around, looking for something or someone else to shoot.

"He shot at Mame." Tom sounded completely surprised.

Long Bill reached up under his hat with his hind paw and gave his brown ear a good scratch. "He never shot at Mame before."

"Now he's askin' for it." Tom pulled his gun from its holster.

Footsteps came from behind them. Long Bill

picked up the sound first. He looked over as Marshal Buck entered the stable from the half-opened door at the back. Finally, Tom's ears heard Buck's movements, and he turned, too. Then a stream of sunlight shone through the opening and hit the marshal's badge, making it gleam.

"I sure am glad I found you two fellas," Buck said, joining them.

Long Bill was equally glad. Calliope's mood was the worst he'd ever seen from him. "I guess you were right about Calliope, Buck." Just then, Bill's ears pricked up as more shots rang out in the street.

"Wooooo-weee! Got me another water barrel!" Calliope shouted.

Tom scowled. "Calliope's out there shootin' up the whole town again, Buck. Now, what're you gonna do about it?" He sounded as if he might be getting a little hot under the collar.

Marshal Buck calmly adjusted his hat. "I don't see that I got much of a choice. I'll have to deputize the both of you."

Long Bill and Tom exchanged surprised looks. *He's kidding, right?* Long Bill thought.

"Raise your right hand." Buck dug into his vest pocket and removed two deputy badges.

Tom put his gun away, then raised his hand.

Marshal Buck dusted off the badges on his shirt-sleeve, then handed one to Tom. He pinned the other one on Long Bill's vest.

"I hereby deputize both of you until this situation is taken care of." Then he nodded at Tom, letting him know it was okay to put his hand down.

"Now, we gotta gather that feller in." The marshal looked at both of his new deputies squarely in the eye. "I know you two have ridden trails with Calliope and put up with his ornery moods. But we've done all the talkin' we can do this time. Now, you shoot just as soon as you get a shot."

"I don't have a gun." Long Bill sat up so they could see that no holsters hung from his hips.

"You keep behind cover and you bring him down," the marshal said to Long Bill as if Longley hadn't said a word. "I certainly wish it hadn't come to this with Calliope, but this time he's gone too far."

More gunfire echoed down Main Street. Buck glanced out the door, then drew his gun.

"It's up to Calliope to turn up his toes this time, I reckon," the marshal said. "And don't be too reckless, boys. What Calliope shoots at—he hits."

Long Bill watched as Tom drew his gun and moved in behind Buck. The marshal's words kept running through his head: *It's up to Calliope to turn up his toes this time.* Why, that meant Buck expected his deputies to shoot Calliope! Sure, Calliope was about as likable as a thief, but kill him? Long Bill didn't think he could do that. And besides . . . "I don't have a gun."

Buck and Tom didn't hear him. They were already edging out the door.

Chapter Twelve

Long Bill leaped down from the barrel to the hay bale. Then he ran across the cool, hard-packed dirt floor of the stable to the door. He followed Tom and Marshal Buck outside, sank to his belly, and crawled along the edge of the building.

One by one, Calliope picked bullets from his cartridge belts and reloaded his guns, swaying as he did. Except for a man riding on horseback at the other end of Main Street, the town was quiet—for the moment.

Who can blame anyone for hiding inside? Long Bill wondered, waiting for Calliope's next move.

When the coast was clear, the marshal motioned to Tom to run ahead. Then nodding to Long Bill to hide behind a nearby water trough, Buck sneaked after Tom.

The sun had already turned hot and was

beating down on Long Bill's fur, making him pant. Suddenly, sensing something odd in the air, he held his black nose high and sniffed. He smelled people—a whole lot of them. Creeping to the edge of the trough, Long Bill peeked out. "Well, I'll be!" he whispered, looking around.

As Calliope continued to reload his many guns, Mame, toting her shotgun, stationed herself on the balcony above her restaurant. Two of her kitchen workers joined her. The barber stood watch on the balcony of the hotel. Below, the real deputy hid between the drugstore and the telegraph office. All up and down the street, the people of Chaparosa were coming out to defend their town.

Long Bill wagged his tail. *When it comes right down to it, they're pretty good people.*

His guns loaded, Calliope looked around. Stretching his neck high and squinting, he took a couple of unsteady steps toward the restaurant. "I see ya up there!" He waved his guns. "You're all gunnin' for the fierce Calliope. But I tell ya—I ain't goin' peaceably! Wooooo-hooooooo!" He leaned back and fired both pistols at the balcony above Mame Dugan's Restaurant. Hats flew off the heads of the two kitchen workers as Calliope hit his marks.

Long Bill pawed his muzzle. "Looks like it's two points for Calliope."

The two workers ran for cover. Mame raised her shotgun, took aim, and fired at Calliope. He jumped out of the way, and her slug hit a pile of horse manure in the middle of the street.

His head held low, Calliope ran onto the restaurant porch to take cover under its wooden balcony. Aiming his guns upward, he shot a number of times right through the balcony floor at Mame.

"Oh!" Mame ran to the other end of the balcony.

Long Bill's ears pointed straight up as more shots rang out from somewhere down the street.

Calliope pressed himself against the building to avoid the steady stream of bullets coming his way. When the gunfire slowed, he leaned out and tried to return fire. But his guns were empty. Diving off the porch, he landed behind the water trough out in front of the restaurant. "You wanna play rough, huh?"

Long Bill could no longer see Calliope. But his sharp hearing told him Calliope was reloading his guns.

"Here we go!" Calliope's head popped up. He shot at the deputy. One of his bullets hit the dentist's sign, which was in the shape of a big tooth. The sign fell, hitting the deputy on the head, knocking him face-first onto the boardwalk.

A bullet whizzed past Long Bill's spotted ear. "Time out!" He ducked his head.

Calliope fired another round of bullets, sending the barber running scared down the stairs from the hotel balcony. Halfway down, he jumped over the railing and landed in a supply wagon parked alongside the hotel.

The gunfire stopped. Calliope looked out from behind the trough. When no one shot at him, he rose and proudly headed for the center of the street.

Long Bill watched George peek out the door of the general store. When no one fired at the storekeeper, George nervously stepped outside to rescue what was left of the china and glassware that had been sitting out front. *Put your thinking cap on, George*, Long Bill thought. *There's a man with lots of gun power out here.*

Calliope aimed in the direction of the store, but instead of hearing a *bang-bang*, Long Bill heard a *click-click*.

Unaware of the danger, George took time to pile his arms higher with dishes.

Calliope threw down his empty guns, crossed

his arms over his chest, and pulled out two more .45's from their holsters. He shot at George again. *Bang! Bang!*

George jumped, dropping the dinnerware. As it crashed to the ground, he ran back inside the store.

Long Bill's tail dropped. "I knew that wasn't a good idea."

A lone tumbleweed rolled across the street in front of the stable. Calliope turned and shot at it. Then he turned back and put holes in two water barrels out in front of the general store.

Licking his lips, Long Bill looked longingly at the water streaming from the barrels. *Water would taste mighty good about now.*

As Calliope swayed and looked for more trouble, Long Bill saw Buck and Tom sneak out from between the laundry building and the undertaker's office. They were directly across the street from him. Ducking behind the water trough, Tom signaled Long Bill with a nod.

Hmm . . . Long Bill looked around. Behind him, on the ground, lay a coil of rope. *Okay. I get it.* He picked up one end of the rope in his teeth and, when Calliope's back was turned, ran it across to Tom.

Calliope turned suddenly, looking in Long

Bill's direction, but Long Bill was hidden safely near Tom.

Ptew! He spat out the rope. *We're going to trip Calliope up!* he thought. A second later, when Calliope turned his back on them, Long Bill raced over to the other side of the street.

Using his mouth, Long Bill picked up the other end of the rope and waited. As Calliope started stumbling backward up the street toward them, Long Bill clamped his teeth tightly around the rope. When Calliope was close enough, Long Bill pulled his end tight, while Tom pulled from the other side of the street.

The rope sprang up. Calliope tripped and fell, nearly landing head-first in a pile of horse dung swarming with flies. Bolting into a roll, he fired a shot, sending Tom ducking for cover behind the undertaker's wooden caskets. He fired again, this time at the marshal. The marshal dodged his bullet by diving into the laundry building. Calliope's third shot came whizzing at Long Bill.

"I don't have a gun!" Long Bill raced behind the water trough. He waited a second, then edged his black nose out. Mame Dugan was ready with her shotgun on the balcony. She fired at Calliope.

Scrambling to his feet, Calliope stumbled

through the pile of horse dung. He ran toward the train station and ducked behind a barrel on the station platform. His movements were slowing down.

Long Bill poked his nose out farther. It looked as if Calliope was losing steam.

The marshal, who was watching from the dark doorway of the laundry building, stepped out and nodded to Tom, who was just a few feet away. The two motioned across the street to Long Bill to join them at the corner.

Long Bill cocked his head and listened for the sounds of Calliope's guns. Hearing nothing, he darted across the street under the cover of a rolling tumbleweed. His heart was pounding when he met up with Buck and Tom at the side of the laundry building.

Marshal Buck reached down to the ground and came up clutching two pieces of straw in his fist. "All right. Draw to see who goes over to the station with me." He held his hand out, offering Tom and Long Bill the straws.

Tom pulled out a straw first. Then Long Bill pulled the remaining one out with his teeth. Measuring the two, and finding his the shortest, Tom sighed.

Long Bill could tell by the look on Tom's face

that Tom was disappointed. Considering that his only weapon was his bark, Long Bill was disappointed, too.

"Well, that's it, then," Buck said to Tom. "Bill and I'll go to the station. You stay here and cover the building in case he comes out."

"Oh, lemme go, Buck!" Tom begged.

"No. Straws have been drawn, Tom." The marshal nodded to Long Bill. "Come on."

"Uh . . . Buck, have I pointed out that I don't have a gun?" Long Bill asked, wagging his tail as he followed Buck.

"Lucky dog . . ." Tom mumbled at their backs.

As Long Bill and Buck looked around the corner of the building, Buck drew his gun.

Helllooo! Does anybody else see what's wrong

with this picture? Long Bill wondered. *I DON'T HAVE A GUN!*

How can Long Bill defend himself? What will happen when he comes face to face with the mean-spirited Calliope?

In the meantime, let's check on the increasingly desperate situation in Oakdale. . . .

Chapter Thirteen

Wishbone sat on the main floor of the *Chronicle* office, near the top of the steps leading down to the archives on the lower level. Leaning over the open newspaper in front of him, he fixed his eyes on a cartoon. "And then the dog says, 'I don't have a gun.'" He wagged his tail. "Ha-ha-ha-ha-ha! Oh . . . that's funny!"

When no one acknowledged him, Wishbone looked down in the archive area at Sam, Joe, and Melina. They were listening to Hank.

Wishbone sighed. "Sometimes they act as if I never say a single word."

"Mr. King *owns* the paper?" Sam asked, bringing one knee close to her chin so she could tie her sneaker. "Where's Miss Gilmore?"

Hank shook his head. He walked to the top of the stairs and looked around the main floor at the employees packing up their personal items. Mr. King would be arriving in a few hours to claim his newspaper. "I haven't seen her since she left earlier today. And I've been digging through the *Chronicle*'s archives ever since, but I still haven't found anything that proves Mr. King wrong."

Wishbone took a step closer to the stairs. "I read the whole comics section. No help there."

"We've been trying to help, too." Joe reached in his back pocket and pulled out the copy of the front-page photo from the twenty-fifth-anniversary edition of the *Chronicle*—the one that Ellen had copied for Sam at the library. He handed it to Hank.

Hank gazed at the picture. "That's my grandfather." Surprised, he looked up at Joe, Sam, and Melina.

Reaching up with both hands, Sam tightened her ponytail. "We thought your grandfather might know something that could shed some light on the situation."

Hank's face brightened. "I never thought of that. Let's go ask him!"

Sam stood up. "Why don't you guys go see him? Melina and I will look in the archives."

"Good idea," Joe and Melina said at the same time.

Hank walked down the steps and handed the

copy of the photo back to Joe. "Come on." He motioned for Sam and Melina to follow him down to the basement. "There are more archives in the basement. I'll show you where. Joe, wait for me by the front door. I'll be right there."

A few minutes later, Joe and Hank walked out the front door of the newspaper office. The Jack Russell terrier was right behind them.

Wishbone trotted happily down the shady, tree-lined street between his two human companions. "This is my favorite kind of walk—good friends, good trees, and no leash!"

"So, you think he'll remember anything?" Joe asked.

Hank shrugged his shoulders. "I don't know. Most of the time he can't remember what he had for breakfast."

Wishbone sprinted into the lead and, a few blocks later, was the first to climb the steps leading up to the porch of Ethan Johnstone's house. Wagging his tail, he walked across the big, covered porch and sat down. He addressed the elderly man sitting in a wooden rocker. "Ethan Johnstone, I presume."

The man had a salt-and-pepper beard and curly gray hair. He was busy twisting half a lemon over the juicer he held in his lap. On the small table beside him was a bowl of lemons and a half-filled pitcher of juice.

"Grandpa?" Hank stepped forward.

Ethan squinted in the direction of the boys. "Who wants to know?" he asked teasingly.

"It's me—Hank."

"Hank?" Ethan teased again.

Joe and Hank exchanged looks of doubt.

"Your grandson," Hank said.

Ethan set the juicer on the table, fumbled in his shirt pocket, and pulled out a pair of glasses. When he put the glasses on and took a good look at Hank, he smiled. "Oh! *That* Hank." He tipped his head in a nod. "He with you?"

Hank looked at Joe. "This is my friend, Joe Talbot."

Joe waved.

"I meant the dog," Ethan said, nodding at Wishbone.

Wishbone smiled a dog smile. "Hank, I think you're wrong about your grandfather. I bet he's like me and remembers *exactly* what he has for breakfast every day."

"Yes, he's with us," Hank said. "His name is Wishbone. He can wait by the bushes—he'll be okay."

"Well, hi, there, little fella." Ethan patted his leg with his hand. "Come on over here."

Wishbone caught a look of surprise passing between Joe and Hank. "I'll handle this, boys." Wishbone trotted across the porch and up to Ethan. He put a paw on the man's leg. "It's like this, Grandpa—Mr. King claims that Wanda doesn't really own *The Oakdale Chronicle*. We were wondering if you could provide us with any information at all that could possibly help . . ." Wishbone leaned toward Ethan's hand as Ethan scratched between Wishbone's ears. ". . . Or you could just scratch my head."

Joe and Hank stepped closer. "We were just wondering if you knew anything about *The Oakdale Chronicle*," Joe said.

Ethan put down his lemon and gave them an odd look. "'Course I know *The Oakdale Chronicle!*" he said gruffly. "It's the newspaper."

Joe pulled out the copy of the front page of the anniversary edition of the paper and handed it to Ethan.

Hank stood beside his grandfather and looked over his shoulder as Ethan checked out the copy of the photo. "Could you tell us what you remember about this picture?"

Ethan continued to study the photo.

"Do you remember the picture, Mr. Johnstone?" Joe asked hopefully.

"Yup. That's me." He pointed to one of the men.

"Right, Grandpa. We just wanted to know if Giles Gilmore really owned the paper."

"Of course he owned it." Ethan poked a finger into the air for emphasis. "Owned it fair and square!" He reached down and patted Wishbone's head. "Didn't he, boy?"

Hmm . . . I think I missed something—like how I should know the answer to that question. "Uh . . . sure," Wishbone agreed.

"His name is Wishbone, sir," Joe reminded him.

"Right. You told me that," Ethan said matter-of-factly. "But I just can't tell you how much he reminds me of my dog, Jack." He handed the sheet of paper back to Hank. Then he leaned to one side

185

and dug his wallet out of his back pocket. "Look at this picture." He pulled out a brown-toned snapshot, creased and worn at the edges. "That's me when I was ten. And that, there, is Jack." He pointed at the dog, then looked at Wishbone again. "Spittin' image."

"We do seem to share the same quality markings," Wishbone said, squeezing in to get a better look.

Hank glanced at his grandfather. "How do you know the *Chronicle* belonged to Mr. Gilmore fair and square?"

Ethan pointed to the paper in his grandson's hands. "Look right there in your picture, Hank!" he snapped.

"Where?" Baffled, Hank held the photo out so he and Joe could study it.

Wishbone stood on his hind legs and rested his front paws on the rocker for a better view.

Ethan tapped the paper. "See, right there on the wall, behind the men."

Wishbone looked closely. "Hmm . . . Looks like a torn piece of paper and a few playing cards framed and hung on the wall."

"It looks like a ragged piece of paper," Joe remarked, squinting.

"That's Gilmore's deed." Ethan rocked his chair.

"'Scuse me." Wishbone took a step back to keep his toes and tail out of the way of the rocker rails.

"On the wall?" Joe looked confused.

Relaxing back into his chair, Ethan stared into space. "I'll never forget that old, torn-up deed. You see, on the night that Gilmore took over the paper from Skelton, he didn't have anything to write on, so they asked me to get something. The only thing I could lay my hands on at the time was an old calendar. So, I tore off a month, they wrote out a deed, and signed it. Gilmore stuck it right up there on the wall."

Joe's face lit up. "Hank—that's it! The proof we need."

"Grandpa, do you think you could help us find it?" Hank asked.

Ethan looked at the boys and smiled. "Well, it has to be at the *Chronicle*. Those Gilmores never threw anything away, especially something that important."

Wishbone scratched his neck. "I don't think Wanda inherited that Gilmore trait. She's always trying to get rid of the bones I bury in her yard."

"So, will you help us, Grandpa?" Hank asked again.

Ethan Johnstone rocked his chair forward and stood up. "Let me go inside and get my hat."

"No need to tell me which way to go," Wishbone said, as he trotted across the main floor of the *Chronicle* office with Joe, Hank, and Ethan. "My nose knows." He paused to sniff, then took off in a trot down the stairs to the archive room. At the bottom of the stairs, Wishbone sniffed again. Then they went down another flight of stairs into the basement.

"Sam! Melina!" Wishbone wagged his tail as he greeted them. "I'm starved. Got anything edible in your pockets?" He sniffed, then sneezed. "Sorry." Wishbone wagged his tail again. "It's not easy for me to cover my mouth. Do you two know you smell a little dusty?"

Joe held the picture out and explained to Sam and Melina about the deed.

Sam examined the photo closely. "Guys, I haven't seen anything that looks like that."

"Me, neither," Melina said. "And we've looked all over this basement, right, Sam?"

"Right."

"Hmm . . . nothing down here," Wishbone said from under a table.

Ethan rubbed his whiskered chin. "It should

be easy to spot, with Gilmore's winning poker hand right above it."

"Poker hand?" Hank echoed.

Ethan nodded and stared out the window toward the sunlight. "It all happened one stormy night about sixty-five years ago. . . ."

"Oh, goody, a story." Wishbone sat on the cool floor under the table and listened. As Ethan talked, Wishbone imagined the whole story. . . .

Chapter Fourteen

As Ethan Johnstone was telling the story, Wishbone imagined Jack, the handsome Jack Russell terrier. Jack was almost as handsome as Wishbone himself, but not quite. It was May 1932 in Oakdale, and a spring rainstorm had been pouring all evening. Ethan, in his black raincoat and rain hat, and Jack in his sleek fur coat, were drenched as they entered the backroom of The Inn. . . .

Four men, one of whom was Ethan's dad, Lee Johnstone, sat around a table playing poker. Another was Abel Skelton, one of the richest men in town. The third man was a stranger. Last, but not least, there was a young upstart named Giles Gilmore. The men wore white shirts with the sleeves rolled up to their elbows, bowties, suspenders, and vests.

Ethan walked around the table, refilling drinks from the pitcher he carried. That was his job for the evening. Water dripped from his raincoat to the floor. Jack followed him, carrying a small, red pail in his teeth by its handle. The pail was filled with peanuts roasted in the shell.

Wishbone was doing such a great job imagining the scene that he could almost smell those peanuts!

"Thanks, Jack," Lee said, taking the pail and setting it on the table.

Jack barked and wagged his tail, but no one gave him a second glance.

Wishbone wagged his tail, too. Come on, guys! Pay attention. He's willing to work for peanuts! Get it? Ha-ha!

Stepping away from the table, Jack shook, ridding his fur of the rain that had settled on it during his walk to The Inn. He looked around for a place to sit.

"Last hand, gentlemen," Giles Gilmore said, as Lee Johnstone dealt out the cards.

Lee Johnstone smiled pleasantly. "The least you could do is let me win one hand before the night is over. Lady Luck has definitely been on your side."

Jack trotted over and jumped up on a stool between Giles Gilmore and Lee Johnstone. It almost

looked as if he wanted to sit in for a hand or two. Ethan came and stood next to him.

Bundles of one-hundred-dollar bills were stacked in front of each man. Jack stretched his neck for a closer look.

Wishbone's heartbeat sped up, just imagining those wonderful-smelling stacks. His tail wagged excitedly. Think of all the chew toys and kibble that money could buy! Whoa! Forget kibble—think prime rib!

"Well, whatcha gonna do there, Giles?" Lee asked Gilmore, who was the man directly to his left.

"I'm going to place a bet." Giles set a small bundle of money in the center of the table. "I'll start with five hundred."

"I'll see it." The stranger added his five hundred to Gile's money, then took a drink.

Abel Skelton glared at Giles Gilmore.

Jack gave Skelton the once-over.

Wishbone knew that Jack, with his keen canine senses, was sensing hostility.

"I'll see your five, and I'll raise you a thousand." Skelton plopped a bigger bundle of money in the center of the table.

With a hefty sigh, Lee Johnstone slapped his cards face-down on the table. "That's too rich for me. I'm out."

"Me, too," said the stranger. He folded his cards together and placed them face-down on the table.

Giles Gilmore stared back at Abel Skelton. "I'll see your thousand," he said calmly, "and I'll raise you five hundred." He tossed $1,500 into the money pot, as if it had no more value than a dried-up bone.

On the surface, Abel looked just as cool and collected as Giles.

You can't fool a dog! Wishbone knew what Jack knew—Skelton was as nervous as a dog on his way to the vet.

"I'll see you . . . and I'll raise you five thousand," Skelton said, using the last of his money. Outside, the storm continued to rage. Wind pelted rain against the high-set windows.

"All right, Abel." Giles nodded. "I'll see your five thousand, and I'll raise you another five thousand."

Outside, thunder crashed and lightning flashed.

Skelton eyed Gilmore. Then his eyes went to Jack. When they did, the dog sat up and begged.

Skelton's face lit up, as if he were taking Jack's begging as a sign. Abel reached into his pocket, pulled out a set of keys, and placed them on the stack of money. "These are the keys to the *Chronicle*. It's not much of a paper right now. But it's gotta be worth at least five thousand dollars." He smiled. "I call."

A slow grin turned up the corners of Gilmore's mouth and crinkled his eyes. He casually spread his cards face up on the table. "A full house— queens over eights."

Lee and the other player chuckled, but Skelton's smile faded. His eyes narrowed into slits as he stared at Giles. "You tricked me. You and that mangy mongrel tricked me!"

Mangy! Mongrel! Wishbone let out a low growl. Jack was a Jack Russell terrier, perhaps the first and noblest breed of dog ever. This Skelton guy must need glasses!

"Now, now, Abel." Lee Johnstone held up a hand to protest. "Your luck's been running muddy all night. Giles beat you fair and square. Besides, the dog belongs to Ethan, here." He looked at his son. "Ethan, why don't you run along and get Mr. Gilmore something to write on so we can write this deal up proper."

Ethan nodded and looked around the room.

Giles Gilmore reached out to collect his winnings from the center of the table. At the same time, Skelton, glaring, reached for the pot, too, trapping Giles's hands beneath his. For a minute the two men didn't move. Finally, Skelton pushed away from the winnings. The tension in that room was as thick as stew.

Ethan hurried over to the wall, where the phone hung. Next to it hung a calendar. Standing on tiptoes, Ethan reached up and ripped off the month of May. He set it on the table, back side up, to show a blank piece of paper. Then he and Jack hightailed it out of there. . . .

Wishbone peeked out from under the table as Grandpa Ethan finished telling his story in the *Chronicle*'s basement.

"And that's how it all ended up," Ethan said. "Skelton moved on to another town, and Gilmore built up the paper into what it's become in modern times."

"That's a terrific story," Joe said.

"So, you see," Ethan continued, "there is no way Gilmore would have lost that deed. He had it framed and everything."

Wishbone trotted over to the group. "What are we standing around here for, people? What we need is some action!"

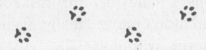

Ethan Johnstone's story just may help save *The Oakdale Chronicle* from the clutches of Leon King—if the kids can find that missing deed.

Meanwhile, back at the ranch—make that the train station—I hope Long Bill can figure out a way to save the town of Chaparosa from Calliope's clutches.

Chapter Fifteen

Long Bill kept a furred side pressed against the corner of the building that housed the laundry. He was hoping to avoid Calliope's bullets. Next to him, Marshal Buck kept peeking out, checking for signs of Calliope. When the coast was all clear, Buck signaled Long Bill with a nod. Then he dashed across the street toward the train station platform.

As Long Bill lit out behind the marshal, shots rang out from Calliope's guns. Long Bill ducked his head, tucked his tail low, and pumped his legs harder. *I think I can. I think I can. I think I can.* His heart pounded to the rhythm of his thoughts.

The marshal jumped onto the platform, rolled, and immediately took cover behind stacked boxes of dry goods.

"Whew!" Long Bill jumped for cover on the second of the three stairs that led up to the platform. Panting, he flattened his underbelly to the hot wooden step, thankful to have a moment to rest.

A distant train whistle pierced the air. Startled, Long Bill almost jumped out of his fur. Calliope fired more shots at them.

The marshal fired back, but Calliope ducked safely behind a water barrel at the other end of the platform. Three horses, hitched to the platform, whinnied as Calliope worked his way closer. Buck nodded at Long Bill, and he gestured with his gun.

Got it. Long Bill wagged his tail to let Buck know he understood. *We're moving in closer.* Stretching his neck, he peeked up over the platform. Then he sneaked to the safety of the closest doorway.

"I see you hightailin' it toward me, Bill," Calliope called. "You'll never catch me."

I must've forgotten to run with my tail down! Long Bill thought.

Long Bill peeked out from the doorway as Calliope made a run for the horses. As Calliope leaned over and untied them, he started to fall forward off the platform. He flailed his arms to

balance himself, but that wild motion and another blast of the train whistle spooked the horses. They ran clear up Main Street. "Hey! Git on back here!" Calliope waved his hands wildly.

Trying to catch Calliope off guard, Marshal Buck openly ran toward Calliope. Calliope drew two more guns and fired.

Dodging bullets, Buck dove toward a hand-cart full of wooden crates and large sacks of grain. He took a deep breath. Then, using the cart as a shield, he rolled it toward Calliope.

Bam! Bam! Bam! Calliope fired off three shots, ripping holes into the sacks of grain.

Looks like a crow's all-you-can-eat buffet, Long Bill thought, as he looked out from the doorway and saw the grain spill to the platform.

His gun ready, Marshal Buck tore around the corner of the cart.

Go, Buck, go! Long Bill silently urged his friend toward cover.

Calliope stood up and fired. His bullet hit a window shutter, flinging it open, smacking Buck hard in the forehead. Buck fell backward onto the grain with a soft thud. His hat popped off and his toes pointed up toward the sky. Buck didn't move.

"Oh, no." Worried for his friend, Long Bill forgot about staying hidden. He rushed toward Buck and called out, "Calliope, look what you did!" He sniffed the marshal's face and was relieved when he heard air whistling in and out Buck's nose.

"Woooooo-hoooooo!" Calliope hooted, pleased with himself. Then he sneered at Long Bill. Just as Calliope started to point his guns in Long Bill's direction, the train chugged into the station and screeched to a stop. Calliope shook his head, as if to clear the noise from his ears. Then he eyed the train with a deadly scowl. All of a sudden, he gasped, as if there were a chicken bone stuck in his throat.

Long Bill glanced down the breezeway between the ticket office and the freight building, toward the tracks. A woman with a tanned, creased face stared back at Calliope through the train window. Her hair was gray. On her head, she wore a saucer-shaped hat covered in different colored flowers.

"Maw?" The color drained from Calliope's face. He looked like a ghost with whisker stubbles and a cowboy hat. And guns!

Calliope's fierceness faded. A look of panic covered his face as he glanced sideways at Long Bill.

"It's my maw!" He holstered his guns, then put one arm up to hide his face. Next, he took a step forward so he was out of her view. "I can't let her see what I've become!" he whimpered.

"Well, it looks like you've gotten yourself into quite a fix, Calliope Catesby," Long Bill said without one whisker's weight of sympathy. It was clear the shoe was on the other foot now. He sat tall by his friend. "Lucky for you the marshal's still breathing."

"Please, Bill—I'm beggin' you!" Calliope's face twisted, as if he'd just gotten a nasty cat bite. "I swear, if you'll give me another chance, I'll quit all my drinkin' and gamblin'. No more gunplay, either. I'll be a good citizen . . . I'll go to work . . . I'll quit my foolishness. I swear, by gum!" Calliope spat on his hand, slapped his heart, then raised his right hand. "Please, Bill—ya just gotta help me. I'll do anything. I'll snort prickly pear cactus up my nose."

"Ewwww!" Long Bill rubbed a paw across his nose as he thought about those needlelike stickers from a prickly pear cactus poking into his snout.

Calliope kept pleading. "I'll dip myself in plum jelly and roll on an anthill. I'll even—"

"Now, hold on just a minute, Calliope." Long Bill held up a paw. "I reckon I've known you for a long time. I guess what it all comes down to is whether I can take you at your word or not."

Calliope and his mother stood on the platform of the train station and looked on as Long Bill nosed the marshal's cheek. "Wake up, Buck." Long Bill nudged him again.

Buck began to groan; his head rolled to one side. Slowly, his eyes fluttered open.

"There, now, you great big strong man!" Calliope's mother smiled down at a confused-looking Buck. "That bullet never even tetched ya! Ya was knocked out by that shutter there, an' it kinda paralyzed ya for a spell. I've heard of this happenin' before." She wrinkled her brows and

thought. "Uh . . . cun—cussion. Yeah, that's what they calls it."

Long Bill tried to signal buck with his tail. He wanted him to look at Calliope—so he'd see what was going on. When that didn't work, Long Bill gave him a hint by scratching his furred chest with his hind paw. But Buck just kept looking around, mostly at the talkative Mrs. Catesby.

"You don't know me, I reckon," she said, adjusting the white, lacy shawl on her shoulders. "I just come in on that train from Alabammy to see my son." She turned and looked proudly up at Calliope. "Just think now, that little ole boy of mine has got to be an officer—marshal of a whole town!" Reaching up, she pulled at the badge pinned to Calliope's chest and pointed it at Buck. It was the badge Long Bill had put there before Mrs. Catesby got off the train.

Nervous as a cat in a doghouse, Calliope looked dumbly at Buck.

Calliope's mother shook her head. "I heard them guns a-shootin' while I was comin' off that train . . ."

Marshal Buck looked at his chest and saw that his badge was missing. Then he looked up at Long Bill.

Bingo! Now you're getting the picture. Long Bill

tried to send silent-thought messages to Buck. *Just play along and everything will turn out fine . . . I think.*

"Listen, you mustn't hold no grudge against my boy for havin' to shoot at ya. He's always been a good boy." Mrs. Catesby continued to speak to Buck. "An officer has got to tend to the law—that's his duty—and them that acts bad and lives wrong just has to pay the price."

Long Bill watched the marshal, hoping he'd play along.

"Won't ya let me give ya some advice, sir?" Calliope's mother leaned toward the ground where Buck lay. "Be a good man, and leave liquor alone. Live peaceable and godly. Keep away from bad company." Her enthusiasm lifted her voice. "Work honest and sleep sweet!"

Buck looked from her to Calliope. "And what does . . . uh . . . 'the Marshal' think about his mother's advice? Does he think it's good advice?"

Long Bill wanted to do a backflip. Buck couldn't have acted out the scene better if he'd been onstage. He was letting Calliope pretend to be the marshal in front of his mother!

With a serious look on his face, Calliope looked Marshal Buck straight in the eye. "I say this—if I was a drunken and desperate character,

I'd follow her advice. And if I was in your place and you was in mine, I'd say: 'Marshal, I'm willin' to swear that if ya give me another chance, I'll be a good citizen. I'll go to work and I'll drop my foolishness. And you have my word on that.'" Calliope paused. "And that's what I'd say to ya if ya was the marshal and I was in your place."

Marshal Buck sat up and touched the lump on his forehead. He checked his fingers, looking for blood—but found nothing. "If you were in my place and you said that, and I was the marshal, I would say to you: 'Go free, and you do your best to keep your promise.'"

A smile the size of Texas crossed Calliope's face. He put an arm across his mother's shoulder and gave her a hug.

Marshal Buck groaned as he tried to stand up. Calliope reached down and gave him a helping hand.

Long Bill saw the look of thanks that passed from Calliope to the marshal. *All's well that ends well,* he thought. He trotted over to Buck's hat, grabbed it in his teeth, and took it to him. "Here you go."

"Thanks, Bill." Buck set it on his head carefully to avoid touching the goose-egg lump that the shutter had given him.

With bullets no longer a threat, the other

passengers began to leave the train. As the folks in town went back to business as usual, Tom strode over and joined Long Bill. Tom must have seen what was going on earlier and figured things out, because he didn't ask a single question.

With a smile, Mrs. Catesby patted Calliope's nicely rounded stomach. "When you goin' ta eat somethin', son? Yer all skin and bones."

"I—"

Suddenly, J. Edgar Todd appeared on the platform and marched toward Long Bill, very businesslike.

With all that was happenin' with Calliope, I completely forgot about my situation with him. Long Bill licked his lips. *This little cat-in-the-grass bank examiner must have been riding on the train.*

"Ah! Mr. Longley, are your affairs in order?" Mr. Todd raised his brows.

"Uh . . . not exactly—"

"There's no use in stalling any longer, Mr. Longley." J. Edgar Todd adjusted his glasses. "The magistrate will be arriving shortly on the stagecoach." He turned to Calliope. "Are you the marshal here?"

Calliope stood there like a tree stump. "Uh . . ." Finally, he looked at Buck, who signaled with his eyes that the bank examiner was talking to Calliope—*Marshal* Calliope. Calliope reached up and shined his badge by rubbing his shirtsleeve on it. Then he shook Mr. Todd's hand.

"Very good, Marshal." The bank examiner looked over his glasses, down at Long Bill. "I need you to arrest this man."

Calliope frowned. His mouth fell open and he showed his yellow teeth. "Long Bill? Ya want me to arrest Long Bill?"

People on the train platform moved about in confusion.

Long Bill sat there silently, looking at the man he'd just helped save face. *What can I say that would help?* he wondered. *Not a dadgum thing, that's what.*

J. Edgar Todd smiled. "Oh, yes. He is to be arrested and taken to the jail. There we shall wait for the magistrate to arrive and settle things." He raised his brows. "Mr. Longley is well aware of the situation."

A gentle breeze blew across the platform. It ruffled Long Bill's fur as Calliope stared at him, still unmoving.

"Well, go ahead, son," Mrs. Catesby urged, "do your duty."

Calliope looked to the marshal, as if silently pleading for direction.

Marshal Buck smiled weakly at him and gave a slight nod of his head, okaying Calliope to make the arrest.

Long Bill sighed. "I tell you, this just hasn't been my day."

Chapter Sixteen

uck walked down the steps leading away from the train station platform and into the sunshine. "Marshal Calliope" and J. Edgar Todd followed; behind them were Long Bill and Tom. The five of them trooped up the street toward the marshal's office.

At the alleyway, Long Bill and the others climbed the stairs to the wooden boardwalk. When they reached the marshal's office, Long Bill jumped up into the chair out front. He breathed in the hot, dry, sage-scented air and waited silently with the others while Buck went inside.

Long Bill tried to look at the bright side of this situation; his tail started to wag but stopped abruptly. *Helllooo! Earth to Long Bill—there* isn't *a bright side to going to jail!*

Buck came out of his office carrying a neck

iron. He hesitated, then handed it to Calliope. "Here you go, Marshal."

In a glance, Long Bill noticed that the looks on Tom's and J. Edgar Todd's faces were as different as night and day. Tom's face was as sad as a hound dog's, while the bank examiner wore a bright-eyed smile on his.

As Calliope placed the iron around Long Bill's neck and locked it, he sighed. "I sure am sorry 'bout this, Bill."

"Great." Long Bill eyed the metal links. "A leash with an attitude."

"Don't worry, Bill." Tom reassured him. "I won't let you go to jail. I'll take your place if it comes to it."

Long Bill looked up the street over his furred shoulder. "I just hope Ed shows up before that magistrate does."

"Uh . . . hold it, Marshal." J. Edgar Todd raised a hand to stop him, then stood watching as the hotel door swung open.

A man in a three-piece suit stepped out. An expensive derby was perched on his head, and he carried a fasionable walking stick in his hand. He looked clean as a cat. Even his white whiskers were well groomed.

"I believe that is the magistrate now." J. Edgar

Todd had the satisfied look of a dog that had just gotten the biggest, juiciest bone. "Excuse me." J. Edgar Todd stepped over to meet up with the man.

Long Bill pricked up his ears and listened.

The bank examiner rounded up the magistrate as if he were a lost steer. He guided him toward the marshal's office. "You're just in time," J. Edgar Todd said. "The marshal, here, was just escorting Mr. Longley into the jail, where we can settle this matter."

The magistrate seemed annoyed. "I could really use something to drink." He turned away from the bank examiner and strode off toward Mame's place.

With a quick glance at the others, J. Edgar Todd turned and followed the magistrate. The bank examiner's smile faded. "Oh . . . uh . . . yes, of course," he said, looking nervous. "We shall join you and conduct our business at the restaurant, then."

As the group followed the bank examiner and the magistrate, Long Bill noticed Tom lagging behind, as if he were the drag rider of this human herd.

Tom caught up with the group just before they climbed the steps to Mame Dugan's Restaurant.

"Listen to all that hootin' and hollerin' going

on in there," Buck said. "It sounds like a pack of wild animals has taken over the place."

Just then, one of the cowboys inside let loose with a big old burp.

Long Bill cocked his head. *Nope. Sounds like a pack of cowboys to me.* He walked under the swinging doors. Then he waited while Calliope pushed through them.

The situation was standing-room-only inside the restaurant.

"This place is as full as a beehive at sundown," Tom said, removing his hat. "Even the piano's being used as a table." He looked quickly around, then let his glance rest on the kitchen doors. "Where's Mame?" he asked over the noise.

But Long Bill was too busy watching out for his paws to watch for Mame. He didn't want any of the boots belonging to the many cowboys shuffling around to come down on one of his padded paws.

As the group squeezed through the crowd to make their way to the counter, Mame pushed through the swinging kitchen doors, carrying three plates heaped with food. Her hair was pulled up on top of her head. But instead of being tidy as usual, her hair had loose strands falling around her flushed face.

"Mame?" Tom called.

As Tom sat down on a newly vacated stool at the counter, his eyes followed her.

All of a sudden the look on Tom's face changed. "For cryin' out loud!"

"What's the matter, Tom?" Long Bill asked, the fur on his neck bristling.

Trying to see around the cowboy hats and heads, Tom stood up. "I'll be right back."

Long Bill thought about following him. But the chain connected to his metal collar reminded him that he was tied to Calliope. "Uh . . . maybe I'll just wait here for you."

Stretching his furred neck, Long Bill watched Tom approach a man sitting alone at a table in the far corner. The man's face hovered low over a plate of food, and his arm worked as fast as it could to shovel the grub into his mouth.

Lucky for Long Bill that his ears were more powerful than those of most folks. He cocked his head and listened through the clattering and laughter at the restaurant.

"Ed?" Tom bent down to get a good look at the man's face. "Ed! When'd you get into town, you devil, you?" Tom was nearly jumping out of his boots for joy.

"I just come on the noon train," Ed said,

picking a pork chop off his plate and chomping into it. Morsels of meat stuck to his cheeks when he pulled the pork chop bone away. "All I could think about the entire way was Mame's fine fixin's." He smiled. "Why, I do believe I could eat myself a steer."

"Well, did you make the deal?" Tom asked anxiously.

Ed nodded and plopped more mashed potatoes onto his plate from the big serving dish on the table. He picked up a white, cloth sack from the floor by his feet and plopped it onto the table. "All bought and sold," he said matter-of-factly. "There's thirty thousand greenbacks in this here sack."

Long Bill howled with delight as he listened to the brothers' conversation.

"Come on, Ed." Tom yanked his brother out of the chair, grabbed the money, and hurried over to J. Edgar Todd at the counter.

"Mr. Todd," Tom said, "this here is my kid brother, Ed." Then he held up the sack. "As you can see, I have more than enough money to cover the loan."

From the next stool over, the magistrate heard what was going on. He stood and glowered at J. Edgar Todd. "Is that what this is all about? You got me out here in the middle of nowhere for this?"

Shrinking down, the bank examiner turned as red as a raw rump roast.

The magistrate looked at Calliope. "Marshal, you may release the prisoner." Then he turned back to J. Edgar Todd. "Don't you ever think before you jump to conclusions?"

"Well, I-I-I . . ." J. Edgar Todd stammered as the magistrate returned to his stool.

Long Bill stood perfectly still, his tail high in the air as Calliope bent down and removed the iron collar.

"There you go, Bill." Calliope gave a sigh of relief as the chain dropped away.

"I'm free?" Long Bill turned to one side of the room, then the other. "I'm free! Free! Free to ride the open range!" He wagged his tail. "Free to watch the sun set and the moon rise! Free to dig—to dig— in the fertile soil of the prairie!" He flipped in the air. "Unleashed! Wha-hooooooo!" Pumping his four legs with all his might, Long Bill raced under the doors of the restaurant and outside to freedom. *"Freeeeeee!"* he barked, chasing after a tumbleweed.

Long Bill is as happy as a pup in a barn full of chew bones.

Things are definitely looking up in Chaparosa. But back in Oakdale, Wanda still has no proof that the *Chronicle* belongs to her.

Chapter Seventeen

Wishbone paced quickly across the basement at *The Oakdale Chronicle*. He was in the middle of giving Joe, Hank, Ethan, Sam, and Melina a pep talk. "Let's shake a leg, people, and find that deed."

Joe glanced around the room, which Sam and Melina had just combed through. "We'll have to spread out and search."

"Bingo! Thanks for listening, Joe," Wishbone said, pleased that his human friend was so good at following simple commands.

Ethan Johnstone pushed up his glasses. "Why don't you boys start with the main-floor office area. I'll nose around the room directly across the hall here and see what I can dig up."

"A word of warning, Grandpa." Wishbone wagged his tail. "When Wanda's around, never

ever say 'dig up.' For some reason those two words seem to upset her. Trust me on this one."

Sam sighed. "You know, this could take forever."

Joe raised his brows. "We don't *have* forever."

"That's for sure," Hank said.

Melina brightened. "How about if I call Marcus and ask him to come over and help us? He's pretty good at snooping around and finding things—even when I *don't* want him to."

"That's a good idea." Joe brushed his hair off his forehead. "We can use all the help we can get."

Wishbone trotted out of the basement behind Joe and Hank. Then he followed them up both flights of stairs to the front-office area. There, Ginny and another employee were answering the telephones. They were the only two employees still around the place.

Jumping up onto a small table against one of the walls, Wishbone looked around. "Nothing here. This corner just seems to be used for storage." He sniffed. "Hey! I smell something." He looked to the stairs leading up to Wanda's office. Leon King stood at the top of the stairs, looking down. "And here it comes now."

"What are you boys doing here?" Leon King

called out gruffly when he spotted Joe and Hank on the main floor below him.

Wishbone circled the table he was on, then jumped down. He put his nose back on duty closer to the floor. "Wait a minute. I just got a whiff of something else." He jerked his head into the air and sniffed again.

Hank tried to explain to Mr. King about Mr. Gilmore winning *The Oakdale Chronicle* in a poker game.

"We're looking for the deed right now," Joe said.

Hank gave the room a quick once-over with his eyes. "It's here—I *know* it."

Leon King was as unfriendly as a cat. "Look, kids, I don't care about any backroom poker game. I just want all of you out of here."

"Wait . . . wait!" Wishbone climbed up on the storage boxes stacked on the floor. He snooped around. "Hmm . . . Look at all this stuff under here. . . . Boxes . . . an old typewriter . . . Hey!"

Wishbone pushed his nose between some boxes to get a better look behind them.

"This desk is missing one leg. And look!" Standing on end, the framed deed supported the legless corner of the desk. "I found it. I found it!"

Wishbone barked. He pulled his head out and looked at Joe and Hank. "Hey, guys! Over here!"

"If you could just give us a little more time . . ." Hank pleaded with Leon King.

Mr. King descended the stairs with a scowl and ushered the boys toward the reception area. "All right, this is enough of your little treasure hunt!" Putting a hand on their shoulders, he pushed them toward the door.

"Hey, guys!" Wishbone barked again. "Helllooo!"

Joe shrugged off Mr. King and turned around. "You have to give Miss Gilmore another chance. She loves this paper!"

Wishbone sighed. "This is exactly what I mean when I say that no one ever listens to the dog. . . . Hey! *Guys!*" he barked louder. "Back here!"

Finally, Joe noticed Wishbone. "What is it, boy?"

Joe and Hank stepped around Leon King and hurried toward Wishbone.

"Hey . . ." Mr. King began to voice his disapproval, but the boys ignored him.

Ginny interrupted Mr. King. "Sir, line two is for you."

"What is it, boy?" Joe asked. He bent and peered under the desk.

"A little thing I like to call . . . a deed!" Wishbone pointed his nose at the item that substituted for the missing desk leg, then barked.

Stooping, Hank tried to see around Wishbone and the other stuff, too. "Look." He nodded. "I think he's found something."

Joe reached between the boxes. "Help me hold the desk up. Whatever it is is under the corner, supporting the desk."

When Hank lifted up the desk, Joe pulled out the framed deed. Joe shoved a nearby book into its place. "Okay, you can let it down now."

Hank set the corner of the desk on the book. Then he stared at the framed deed along with Joe.

"This is it!" Excitement filled Joe's voice as he brushed dust and cobwebs from the frame with his hand. "I can't believe you found it, Wishbone!"

Wishbone sat tall on his haunches. "What's so hard to believe? I'm a dog of many talents—*when I'm not on a leash!*"

"Come on!" Hank said. "Let's go show Mr. King!"

As Joe, Hank, and Wishbone hurried his way, Leon King hung up the phone.

"See! This is it!" Joe held out the deed. "This proves Miss Gilmore owns *The Oakdale Chronicle*."

Mr. King took the frame and examined the deed. He raised a brow. "Look, kids, for all I know, *anyone* could have written this up. To make this a binding document, what you really need—"

". . . is a witness," Ethan Johnstone said from behind them.

They all turned. Next to Ethan stood Sam and Melina, dusty from the archives, but smiling.

Ethan frowned through his glasses. "Leon King, is that you out here causing trouble?" He stepped forward. "Why, if your father were alive . . ."

Mr. King looked around nervously. "Mr. Johnstone, I didn't know you were here."

"Lucky for Wanda Gilmore and these kids that I am." He shook his head. "Trying to take away her newspaper. I remember you taking away your little brother's toys. I guess you haven't changed much." Ethan sounded disgusted.

"You tell him, Grandpa!" Wishbone wagged his tail.

Mr. King tried to explain. "Now, look, I—"

With a quick wave of his hand, Ethan cut him off. "Here's the truth of the matter: Wanda has a deed, the deed has a witness, and you . . ." —he paused to poke a finger at Leon King—". . . don't have a newspaper. So, why don't you just go on and get out of Wanda Gilmore's *Chronicle* building." He grabbed the framed deed out of Leon King's hand.

Mr. King forced a small laugh. His face reddened. "All right, mister, I—"

Ethan cocked his head and raised a threatening finger in the air.

Leon King sighed. *"Grandpa,"* he said reluctantly. "Grandpa. You win." He started backing up toward the front door. "You win." He picked his suit jacket off the back of a nearby chair and hurried out the door.

"Good-bye, and good riddance!" Wishbone barked.

A smile spread across Joe's face when the door shut behind Leon King. "That's great! Now Miss Gilmore's got her paper back!"

"She never lost it," Ethan said, as Melina and Sam moved closer. "The only problem is, we're the only ones who know that at the moment."

Hank looked at them as if they'd all forgotten where they'd buried their favorite squeaky toys. "Hey, guys, this is a newspaper!" he reminded them. "We can get the word out to everyone in Oakdale in the paper's morning edition."

"And I'm a dog who would gladly accept a reward for finding the newsworthy deed," Wishbone said. "Anything edible would be fine. Cookies, potato chips, steak . . ."

Ginny walked up to the group and smiled. "It sounds like you mean to put out a paper. Count me in."

"Good." Joe smiled. "Where should we start?"

"With the dog's reward," Wishbone said.

"I'll call my dad, and he can call your mom," Sam said. "I'm sure they'll want to help, too. I'll take photos of the deed." She smiled. "Maybe my dad will bring some pizza."

Wishbone wagged his tail. "Okay. Let's start with Walter."

Later that evening, Ellen, her arms filled with

grocery bags, tried to open the door to the *Chronicle's* offices.

"Ellen!" Wishbone greeted her happily as Marcus opened the front door and let her into the bustling offices.

"Thanks, Marcus." Ellen carried a big grocery bag in each arm. A bag of potato chips dangled from her fingers.

Wishbone wagged his tail. "Party time! Need me to take those chips off your hand, Ellen? Just slip the bag between my teeth."

She passed one of the grocery bags to Marcus. "I'm sure everyone's getting hungry. Maybe you could find a spot for these snacks."

"Okay." Marcus walked toward an empty table. Ellen followed him.

"Hey! Wait for me!" Wishbone bolted after them.

Joe waved to Ellen from Wanda's open office above. He was sitting at Wanda's desk, talking on the phone.

As Ellen and Marcus passed Ethan Johnstone and Ginny, the two looked up from the laptop computer that they were sharing, writing a story together. They smiled.

"Refreshments!" Wishbone informed them excitedly.

227

Ellen and Marcus put the food down on the empty table.

All of a sudden, Wishbone turned away from the table, his nose in the air. "I smell pizza!" He spotted Sam's dad near the front door, his arms piled with Pepper Pete's pizza boxes.

Wishbone raced over to round him up. "This way, Walter!"

Wishbone led Walter to the food table. Then Wishbone hung around until someone tossed him some pizza. "Mmm-mmm. I love a work party," he said, licking cheese from the roof of his mouth. "Friends helping friends. What more could anyone ask for? Hey, Melina, how about a few of your chips?"

Melina turned away to talk to Hank, who was at a large desk doing a page layout. "Can I pick out the picture of Miss Gilmore to use in the paper?"

"Sure." He handed her a box of photos.

As Melina sorted through the pictures, Marcus came and stood by her side. "I want to help Miss Gilmore, too," he said. "What can I do?"

Melina looked up, but she didn't say anything.

"Two heads are better than one." Wishbone wagged his tail. "Unless there's only one bone up for grabs."

Finally, Melina smiled at Marcus. "You can help me."

"Thanks!" Marcus eagerly began to examine the photos with his sister.

Wishbone trotted up the stairs that led to Wanda's office and his best friend. "If this is going to be a late night, there are a few things I'll need, Joe—a comfortable place to nap, snacks, water, snacks, a toy so I don't get bored . . . and, oh, did I mention snacks?"

Chapter Eighteen

Wishbone, Joe, Sam, and Hank were all up early Thursday morning. So were the others who had worked on the paper the night before, plus a few more kids. They waited eagerly on the sidewalk in front of the *Chronicle* building. Everyone but Wishbone wore a brightly colored *Chronicle* T-shirt.

Wishbone wagged his tail. "I think it's neat that all of you guys have on a team shirt." He looked up at Joe. "How come the dog didn't get one?"

Sunshine glinted off windows as a delivery truck rumbled up Oak Street toward them. The truck stopped in the middle of the street and the driver jumped out. He hurried around to the back of the truck. The large door rattled as he pulled it open.

"Wow!" Wishbone wagged his tail as he jumped off the curb and peered inside. "Look at all those newspapers—the whole truck is filled!"

Joe followed Hank as he stepped up to the back of the truck and pulled out a paper. Sam and Wishbone crowded around them. Together they looked at the front-page headline. Joe read it out loud:

"GILMORE OWNS AND RUNS PAPER
FAIR AND SQUARE!"

Joe's eyes dropped below the headline to the tag line, which he also read out loud: "This edition of the *Chronicle* was put together entirely by the citizens of Oakdale, without the express knowledge of Wanda Gilmore."

Included on the front page was a picture of Wanda, wearing a big smile and a striped hat.

Others crowded around.

"That picture looks great," Ginny said.

"Yeah," a kid in a blue T-shirt agreed.

Smiling, Marcus and Melina gave each other a high-five.

"Okay, everybody," Hank said, gesturing. "Let's get an assembly line going from here to the sidewalk. We need to get these bundles of newspapers unloaded." He nodded to his right. "We'll stack them up there."

Sam stepped up behind Hank. She took a bundle of papers from him and passed it back to Joe. "Here you go."

Joe smiled and passed the bundle to Marcus.

"Many hands make light work," Wishbone said. He stepped back and watched the newspapers being passed from Marcus all the way to the end of the line. "But since I don't actually have hands, I'll just supervise." He walked up and down the human assembly line for a few minutes, watching the bundles move from hand to hand. Then he bounded to a sunny spot near the front doorway and lay down.

With the line in full swing, and twelve stacks of papers sitting on the sidewalk, Joe stepped out

of place. "Okay," he called. "We need people on the sidewalk to cut the cords on the bundles and roll and rubber-band the papers individually."

Kids who weren't busy unloading the truck stepped over to a bench on the sidewalk in front of the *Chronicle* building. They started banding the newspapers.

Ginny walked by and smiled. "Great!"

Wishbone watched as kids lined up to fill their bike baskets with newspapers, then pedal off. When a number of kids had gone on their way, he squeezed in between the remaining legs and bike tires. "Excuse me. Dog coming through." He pushed his way to the bench, grabbed a rolled-up paper in his teeth, and trotted up the street.

The town was beginning to wake up. People were out and about. In fact, Leon King was just ahead of Wishbone, strolling up the sidewalk in front of Beck's Grocery.

Wishbone watched as Leon King, dressed in a suit, paused at a row of streetside metal newspaper dispensers. The man glanced up the street slyly. When no one was looking, he banged on the rack so that it opened. Smirking, he removed a paper.

"That's dishonest," Wishbone said. He trotted past the well-dressed Leon King. "Definitely—you can't judge a book by its cover!"

Just past Beck's, Wishbone cut across the street to some houses.

"Good shot!" he called to a kid in a yellow Oakdale *Chronicle* T-shirt who tossed a newspaper from his bike to a porch mat.

Wishbone aimed his nose toward the Talbots' cul-de-sac. *Almost there . . . almost there . . . almost there.* The nearer he got to home, the faster he ran.

With only a glance at his house, Wishbone made a beeline to Wanda's porch. Empty flowerpots were strewn about. There sat Wanda, on a porch step, staring at her hands. Her face was solemn. She was wearing her blue robe, and weaving string in and out of her fingers.

It's worse than I thought—she's playing Cat-in-the-Cradle! Oh, poor Wanda. Leon King has really gotten to her! Standing on his hind feet and leaning his front paws on her knees, Wishbone dropped the latest edition of *The Oakdale Chronicle* into Wanda's lap. "Feeling a little low, I see. This should bring a smile to your face."

"Hello, Wishbone," Wanda said without any enthusiasm. She reached out and picked up the rolled-up paper, then looked at it, puzzled.

"No doggie tricks. I promise." Wishbone wagged his tail. "Open-open-open!"

Removing the rubber band, Wanda unfolded

the paper and rested it on her lap. She began to read the front page aloud: "'This edition of the *Chronicle* was put together entirely by the citizens of Oakdale . . .'"

"And the cute canine," Wishbone interjected.

"'. . . without the express knowledge of Wanda Gilmore. It has been compiled by freelance reporters doing an independent investigation . . .'" A smile slowly spread across Wanda's face. When she looked at Wishbone, she was beaming.

Wishbone gave her his best doggie smile in return.

"Wishbone, would you care to join me for

breakfast?" she asked happily, reaching out to scratch his head.

"Oh, yes! I always have room for another breakfast."

Stuffing the paper under one arm, Wanda got up and opened her front door.

Wishbone led the way inside. "You don't have kibble for breakfast, do you, Wanda? . . . Well, if you don't, that's okay. Eggs would be nice, then—scrambled, please, and make sure that there's no pepper on them."

It was almost sunset. Wishbone was curled up in his big red chair in the study, relaxing. Ellen was at her desk next to him, tapping away on her keyboard.

The doorbell rang. Wishbone lifted his head. "Would you get that, please, Ellen? Joe's outside shooting hoops, and I've been up since the crack of dawn."

Ellen pushed the Save key on her keyboard. Then she went out of the room and opened the front door. "Wanda! Hi." Smiling, Ellen opened the door wider. "Come in."

When Wanda stepped into the front hall, Wishbone saw she was wearing a bright blue blouse and skirt, and her flowered sneakers. On her head was blue straw hat with brightly colored flowers all the way around the brim.

"Now, *that's* the Wanda we know and love," Wishbone said, without even lifting his head.

"I'm so touched by what Joe and the other kids did for me that I can't sit still." Her hands gestured through the air as she talked.

Ellen smiled. "Oh, Wanda, you mean so much to everyone in Oakdale. I'm sure the kids were glad to be of help."

"Well"—her hand went to the brim of her hat—"since Wishbone was the one who found the deed, I thought I'd see if he'd like to go for a walk. It's sort of my way of showing my appreciation."

"Never too tired for a walk." Wishbone was on his feet and in the entryway in a flash.

"I think that's Wishbone's way of saying 'yes.'" Ellen opened the door and let them out. "'Bye."

"Actually," Wishbone said, as he trotted up the street next to Wanda, "my way of saying 'yes' is to say 'yes.' But nobody ever listens."

They walked for a while without speaking.

Wishbone sniffed his way up a section of the sidewalk. "Ooh! Gum!" He tried to lick it up, then gave up. Raising his head, he continued on. "It's a beautiful evening, isn't it, Wanda? Hey . . ." He cocked his head. "I hear something. And I think it's coming from Snook's Furniture."

Wishbone trotted faster.

"Come on, Wanda. Don't you think it's neat that they have more than one television?"

Wishbone thought about the other times he'd stopped at Snook's.

"I don't know . . . sometimes those sets just seem to suck you right into whatever's on."

Wishbone sighed when they reached Snook's and looked in the front window at the televisions.

"Oh. It's *her* again," he said, looking at the news anchorperson on the screen. "But this time she has the look of a cat stuck in a tree."

"Good evening," the anchor said. "This is Helen Davidson for Fast News Fifty-seven. It has been brought to our attention that there were several incorrect statements in Mitch McCain's investigative report on Wanda Gilmore. . . ."

"I'll say!" Wanda raised her eyebrows.

"Aha!" Wishbone pawed the air. "I knew she looked cornered."

On screen, Helen Davidson glanced down at the sheet of paper on her desk, then continued. "We seriously hope that our comments and statements did not offend Wanda Gilmore, or anyone in the Gilmore family." She turned over the paper in front of her. "And now, here's Mitch McCain with part one of his week-long exposé: The Dewey Decimal System: A Secret Alien Code—Fact or Fiction?"

Wishbone wagged his tail. "Now, there's an assignment that's out of this world."

The camera switched to Mitch McCain. "Thank you, Helen."

Smiling, Wanda slowly shook her head and walked away. "Come on, Wishbone, I've heard all I want to hear from Fast News Fifty-seven. Let's get some more exercise."

"You know, Wanda," Wishbone said, getting in step with her, "I think we need to do a news piece on something really important. An important political issue. Something that concerns every American citizen's basic rights of freedom and happiness." There was a real bounce in his step. "I want to call it: Abolishing Leash Laws—the Right Thing to Do!"

All's well that ends well in Oakdale. Friends helping friends has paid off in a big way.

Let's see if that holds true for the Wild West town of Chaparosa. . . .

Chapter Nineteen

A week had passed since the magistrate had come to town and Long Bill had been cleared of any wrongdoing concerning Tom's loan.

Long Bill sighed contentedly as he trotted across the dirt street toward the cheerful yellow siding of Mame Dugan's Restaurant. He was wearing his chaps and vest and cowboy hat—and did that ever feel good! He paused to give himself a shake—his way of adjusting his neckerchief.

Long Bill trotted under the swinging doors that led into the restaurant. He crossed the floor and jumped up to his regular stool between Tom and Buck, who were waiting for their food. "Howdy," he said above the familiar eating noises. Already the place was filled with hungry men gulping down their chow.

Buck nodded his hello. "Howdy, Bill," Tom said, sporting a big grin.

Mame looked out from behind the kitchen doors. "The special for you, Bill?"

He put his black nose in the air and sniffed. "Mmm-mmm. Whatever it is I smell will be fine." He sat back on his haunches and relaxed. "Whew! Another day done at the bank. All I've got left to work on now is my appetite."

The doors leading from the street swung open. Tom, Buck, and Long Bill turned to look. Calliope trudged inside and up to the counter.

"I'm plumb tuckered out," Calliope said, as he collapsed onto the stool next to Buck. He set his hat on the empty stool next to him. "I just put maw on the train back to Alabamy." Pulling the badge from his worn shirt, he slapped it on the counter in front of Buck. "Here. I can't take bein' marshal no more—it's too much responsibility!"

Long Bill put a paw on the counter. "Does this mean you'll be returning to your former ways, Calliope?"

"Oh, no. Uh-huh." Calliope shook his head, as if he were trying to get a flea out of his ear. "No, sir. Nope."

"Calliope . . ." Tom and the marshal said at the same time. Both looked at him, disbelieving.

"I learned my lesson," Calliope assured them.

Well, you can *teach an old dog new tricks,* Long Bill thought.

Mame pushed through the kitchen doors carrying three big plates of food, one in each hand. "Here you go, Bill."

When she set a plate down in front of him, he immediately started lapping at the potatoes and gravy. "Mmm-mmm. Never been better, Mame."

Mame set a plate down in front of Buck. Then she gave the third one to Calliope. "This one's yours. I heard you talking, Calliope, and I thought I'd bring you a special."

"Thank you, Mame," Calliope said.

When Mame didn't hurry back into the kitchen, Long Bill looked up.

Mame was looking at Tom and noticing his place was empty, except for a cup. She tilted her head. "Tom? You don't want anything to eat?"

Tom looked as calm as a puddle on a windless day. "Ah, no, Mame. I think I'll just stick with coffee."

Slowly, a smile spread across Mame's face. Not just a "that's nice" smile, but a warm smile meant *just* for Tom. And her eyes were locked on his, as if there wasn't one other person in the noisy room.

Long Bill dropped his muzzle back to his plate

and continued to enjoy his food. *Turning down these tasty tidbits—now, that shows willpower! It must be love.* Just as Long Bill was licking up the last of his meal, he was approached from behind.

"Bill?"

Long Bill turned to see George and several cowboys. His tail wagged once across the stool. "George."

George looked a little nervous. "I was wonderin' if we could talk to ya about somethin' of a business nature."

"Why, sure, George." Long Bill licked his lips clean. "Ya'll come on by the bank next week. I'll be glad to talk to ya. Right now, though, I think I'm gonna take me a short break from the banker's life and head on back out to the range." Aiming his black nose at the floor, Long Bill jumped down from his stool. With a wag of his tail, he walked eagerly under the swinging doors to the great outdoors.

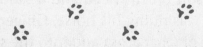

The Old West has a special place in our imaginations. From this rugged new territory came folk heroes who lived on the frontier—a frontier where freedom was cherished and

people lived their lives by a simple code of honor. O. Henry captured the heart of the West for all time in his short stories—full of colorful characters and surprise endings that stick to our ribs for a long time. Why, I'd give my favorite chew bone for a chance to talk to O. Henry!

So Wishbone imagined himself as a cowboy with a Stetson on his head and a saddle beneath his tail. He was riding his horse, Ginger, down the main street of Chaparosa and into the sunset. And riding by his side was the famous author, O. Henry.

"So, Mr. Henry . . . may I call you 'O'? . . . Thanks. You know, I have my own idea for a story. It's about a dog—not just any dog. It's about a dog—and he talks! Well, okay, he talks, but nobody really pays him any attention. *Nobody ever listens to the dog.* That's one of the things he says all the time. And he has this big imagination, and all the time he's finding himself in these incredible stories. Like . . . uh . . . one time, he's an orphan; and another time, he's a great detective; and another time, he's a cowboy! And I've been working on my cowboy yell. Listen to this: Whoo-wee! Heh-heh-heh-heh. Anyway . . . uh . . . I'll give you the short version. Okay? O, are you listening?"

About O. Henry

The most popular short-story writer in American literary history is O. Henry. He wrote approximately 300 short stories during his life. More often than not, his stories ended with a surprise—an unexpected twist. He is known as the author who introduced the surprise ending, a style that has been a delight to many readers.

O. Henry was born in Greensboro, North Carolina, in 1862. His real name was William Sydney Porter. He used a dozen pen names—fictitious names—before he decided on O. Henry.

At the age of nineteen, O. Henry (still known as Will Porter) left his job as a pharmacist in his uncle's drugstore in Greensboro and went to Texas. He learned all about ranching, including riding, roping, and herding sheep. These abilities later helped to flavor his stories set in the Southwest. Tales that he heard from the cowhands about their real lives, as they all sat around the evening campfires, more than likely inspired some of O. Henry's stories.

Life was seldom easy for O. Henry. He had married at age twenty-five; ten years later his wife died of tuberculosis. Just before her death, he was accused of stealing money from the First National Bank of Austin, Texas, where he worked as a teller. O. Henry fled to Honduras, a country in Central America. He returned later to the U.S. to serve a five-year prison sentence. Although he had been found guilty of the crime, O. Henry always denied the charges. Even the bank doubted that he was guilty. Some people thought O. Henry was a victim of the loose banking practices that went on during that time. Could that be where the idea for his story "A Call Loan" came from?

Going to prison gave O. Henry time to write, as well as providing him with ideas for his stories. From the other prisoners he heard about the adventures of Texas outlaws.

O. Henry's first story was accepted for publication in 1897, when he was thirty-five.

O. Henry's stories have been translated into ten languages. One of the most famous of all of his stories is "The Gift of the Magi." He died in 1910, a few years after it was published.

About *Heart of the West*

Heart of the West is a collection of short stories written by O. Henry. It was published in 1907. Three of the stories from this collection inspired the writing of *Wishbone's Dog Days of the West*. The stories are "A Call Loan," "The Reformation of Calliope," and "Cupid à la Carte." Characters, settings, and story lines from these three tales were blended, cut, and shaped to give the reader an overall sampling of O. Henry's writing.

O. Henry wrote about places where he'd lived. The material for *Heart of the West* came from the time when the writer lived in Texas for fourteen years. He spent time in La Salle County (a hundred miles south of San Antonio), and in the cities of Houston and Austin. He was a rancher, draftsman, bank teller, and drugstore clerk. O. Henry also started his own newspaper, *The Rolling Stone*, which lasted only one year.

About Vivian Sathre

Vivian Sathre didn't always know she wanted to be a writer. In fact, she was married and had three children before she knew it! Before becoming an author, she worked as a keypuncher, a bank teller, and a computer-tape librarian. She loves writing and hopes to stay a writer forever. And, like Wishbone, she enjoys curling up with a good book and a good snack.

Vivian Sathre grew up as the youngest member of her family, with four older brothers and two sisters. They almost always had a dog, but none that could speak as clearly as Wishbone.

Vivian has written a number of books for young readers, including picture books, chapter books, and books for middle-grade readers. *Wishbone's Dog Days of the West* is her third WISHBONE book. She also wrote *Dog Overboard!* and *Digging Up the Past*.

She lives in the Seattle, Washington, area with her husband, Roger, her two teenage sons, and two cats.

Coming Soon!

The SUPER Adventures of WISHBONE

The Legend of Sleepy Hollow

By Carla Jablonski

Inspired by "The Legend of Sleepy Hollow" by Washington Irving

Now Playing on Your VCR...

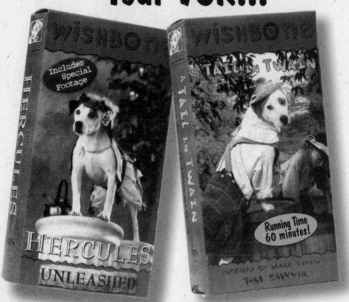

Two exciting **Wishbone**® stories on video!

Ready for an adventure? Then leap right in with **Wishbone**™ as he takes you on a thrilling journey through two great action-packed stories. First, there are haunted houses, buried treasure, and mysterious graves in two back-to-back episodes of *A Tail in Twain*, starring **Wishbone** as Tom Sawyer. Then, no one is more powerful than Hercules...or rather **Wishbone**, in *Hercules* Unleashed, featuring exciting new footage! It's more fun than a flea dip! It's **Wishbone** on home video.

Available wherever videos are sold.

SWEEPSTAKES RULES